TEASE:
THE LACE COLLECTION

TEASE: THE LACE COLLECTION

FRANK LEE SPEAKING

DEDICATION PAGE

I would like to dedicate this book to my parents, my grandmother, Louvenia Webber and family and friends that helped, inspired, and supported me during this entire project.

This book is also in memory of my grandmother, Avolia Howard, who passed away back in 2008. She will forever be in my spirit and serve as a key storyteller in my life.

Acknowledgements

I would like to thank all the contributors to this book for their time and expertise. I am grateful for your creative energy for this project from the beginning to its completion.

I am very grateful to my family for tolerating my neglect while finishing this book. I also want to express my appreciation to all of my friends.

Finally and foremost, I want to thank my cousin and lifetime friend, Danny Howard, who has seen me through my rollercoaster ride of successes and failures.

TABLE OF CONTENTS

WRITING

June 2, 2014

I WROTE MY THINKING down so you could read my thoughts.

I want words that inspire, shape, stretch me beyond my limits and expand my horizons so I can reach them.

I want to feel life's winds upon my face like the swirling winds on a mountaintop or embrace the mist of the rising tide boldly colliding with the jagged rock.

Words are the raw pieces; the pen is the tool of remediation for blank pages; and my thinking is the architect.

My words are verbal therapeutic gifts to encourage, empower, uplift and inspire.

Poets are verbal doctors that massage your intellect; apply ointment and bandages to your emotional scares; raise your awareness of unhealthy relationships; and give you medicine for a broken heart, disappointment, discouragement, and

everyday frustrations.

Poets give you a temporary off ramp to the road to insanity.

Poets don't make you better; we make you stronger!

THE SECRET BEHIND THE TRUTH

"MOM, THE LIGHTS won't come on this morning. Did we have a power outage?" her oldest son said.

Betty hurriedly got out of bed to check. She looked out the window and saw lights on in the neighbor's houses. She called the electric company to report the problem.

"Ma'am, your services have been disconnected due to non-payment." Betty was hurt and outraged as furious thoughts raced through her head.

"Damn Lee! I'm so sick of struggling to get by from day to day. Why didn't you pay the light bill?" as she slammed her fist on the table.

"Momma, are you ok?" as her oldest son peaked into her bedroom.

"No but I will work it out." she replied as she held back tears. She called a friend to borrow the money to get services restored.

Pearson Caldwell came from extremely poor beginnings. He was the youngest of five children from a broken home. Pearson's parents divorced when he was 3 years old. His father worked out of town as a truck driver. Based on the contentious relationship between his parents, Betty and Lee, Lee spent little time with his children. Pearson's parents constantly fought over money and infidelity. Betty often accused Lee of "sleeping around," leading the life of a single man. Gossip about Lee leading this lifestyle was probably true. Lee loved the "fast" life but he also loved his children. However, he had an odd way of showing his affection, based on his lack of involvement in his children's lives. He thought that as long as he provided food to eat and a place to stay, he met his parental obligations. Lee was sadly mistaken. Often the victim of a money making scheme, Lee made poor financial decisions, putting his family's livelihood at risk. On many occasions, Lee gambled away the family's food money on a get-rich scheme that never materialized. After many years of financial instability and contentious arguments, Betty reached her breaking point and filed for divorce. She wanted out. She had endured enough marital struggling and suffering. Unfortunately, things didn't get any better after the divorce. Betty was a single mother of five small children, all under the age of fifteen. She still struggled to provide for her family. Pearson saw his mother struggling financially and vowed he would help.

"Mommy, I'm going to make a lot of money one day so you won't have to work so hard or worry about where our next meal is coming from," he professed to his Mother at the ripe old age of thirteen.

"I'm going to be a successful businessman. With all this modern technology, I'm bound to make something out of my life. I know I can do it," he said.

These were bold words from a thirteen year old. She thought that it was sweet her youngest son wanted to help with the family's expenses.

Growing up, Pearson was a smart and savvy young man. He had the "street hustling" skills of his father and the work ethic of his mother. He remembered what his mom told him: 'Change your thinking one thought at a time. Change your life one day at a time.' Betty used to say these words to motivate and encourage her children. Each day before she started her busy work routine, she kissed each one of her children giving them a positive thought for the day. She would say, "Life gives you crayons, it's up to you to decide how you color the pages or if you color inside the lines." Pearson never figured that quote out until he became a man.

Initially, Pearson held bitterness and resentment toward his father. After the divorce, his father rarely visited, called or spent any significant time with any of his children. He saw the divorce as a "free pass" to live the "fast" life. Betty would often sit Pearson down and have talks about his bitterness.

"Pearson, you can't go through life being bitter toward your father. He made a choice. We all have choices in life." She said.

"He left and hasn't really been back. He wasn't here much when you guys were married. I really don't expect to see him now. What a deadbeat!"

"Don't ever disrespect your father. He is still your father regardless of how you feel about him. Even thought we aren't together, there are good things about him I want you to see. You may not right now but hopefully; you will see what I mean later in life. One day you may be a parent. You need to set a good example.

We all have choices and make decisions in life. Being a good man involves respecting your parents regardless of your relationship with them." She calmly explained.

"I know momma. It just hurts." He muttered.

"I know son. You will find you way. You are a good young man. I know you will do well in life." as she held back her tears.

* * *

Pearson excelled in academics and sports. His mother always told him, "You may lose your talents but your education last a lifetime." Pearson took that statement to heart. With limited financial means, Pearson used sports as an avenue to earn his education. He never forgot the promise he made to his mother when he was thirteen. He understood her sacrifices in taking care of her family. In his mind, Pearson was going to be a businessman.

Pearson was keen in science, mathematics and computers. He spent countless hours at the library studying, reading, and learning things to quench his curiosity for technology. When he wasn't excelling in track and field, he was busy figuring out how to make extra money. He created many small businesses throughout high school and into his first years of college. From lemonade stands to dog walking ventures and everything in between, he was constantly looking for a new opportunity. His perspective was to discover an unfilled need and develop a solution—for a price of course.

Unlike his father, Pearson learned valuable money management lessons from his grandmother. Unlike most teenagers his age, Pearson spent his money wisely. While most of his friends were working to make extra money for pleasure and entertainment, Pearson's money goals were more enterprising. Willing to take chances, he was a visionary at an early age. He wanted to build wealth and was willing to sacrifice temporary gratification for long-term rewards. His love would always be in technology; however, he spent many hours reading the Wall Street Journal.

"I'm going to be the Wizard of Wall Street," he would often say. His friends often laughed. Garrett was one of Pearson's best friends in high school. "P" as Garrett often called him, "when are you going to wake up and stop dreaming?"

"You don't know anything about stocks and you barely have 15 cents over bus fare", Garrett often said.

"Maybe for now, but I'm learning a lot and it's just a matter of time," Pearson retorted.

Pearson was a natural at learning technology and business. His gregarious personality made him popular both inside and outside the classroom. Since math was one of his strongest subjects, he set up a tutoring business in college to help other students struggling with their courses. He knew that the average incoming freshman acclimated slowly to the fast pace of college. These same students were quite unfamiliar with who to talk to and how to ask for help. Pearson used data mining methods to consolidate and track student information. He contacted the math and science professors to let them know he was available to help students, and applied some common sense marketing techniques by visiting the freshman dorms and passing out flyers to prospective customers at the beginning of each semester.

His tutoring business grew from a one-man show to a 20-person operation with dozens of customers. Soon, Pearson wasn't doing any of the marketing or tutoring. His primary role was coordinating and overseeing his entrepreneurial venture. The additional income came in handy as he often sent money to his mother. She was surprised to receive a check in the mail. Sometimes smiling to herself, she was proud her son kept his promise. The success of the tutoring business brought popularity, especially with women on campus. Although he was physically appealing as an athlete, Pearson was more popular for his charismatic and dashing personality. Standing 6'3" tall with broad shoulders and a slender waist, Pearson looked more like a head-turning model then a sprinter. He had an excellent physique for someone that spent limited time in the gym.

With his magnetic popularity, women came and went in Pearson's life. As a young adult, he experienced college life to the fullest. Although he never joined a fraternity, he dated his share of sorority women. Pearson came into his own as a man. He went from being a "caterpillar" to a "lion" between the sheets. Sarah, Mary, Carolyn, Misty, and Susie were just a few women that Pearson had his way with in his off campus apartment. He was sexually promiscuous. However, Pearson did date one woman for a couple of years but he ended the relationship when he graduated. She wanted to get married; he wanted to explore the world. He felt he was too young to get married. Instead, he did what most hot-blooded young men in college did: have a lot of sex.

Prior to his May graduation, Pearson had multiple job offers. However, unexpectedly, he chose the military option. The military offered him a huge sign-on bonus based on his technical acumen. It was the possibility to travel that swayed his decision. He always wanted to explore the world. All of his friends were shocked that he chose the Armed Services route.

""P" what are you doing man?" Garrett said when he heard the news. "You—in the military; I had no idea you even considered that as an option. What about all the Fortune 500 companies that were recruiting you—almost begging you to work for them?"

"Garrett, I thought about the corporate route, but I wasn't interested. There's just too many politics. Besides, I want to travel. They said if I joined, I will become an officer—whatever that means."

I'm still having a hard time seeing you in a uniform. You don't seem like the type but if you think it'll work for you, I will support you. Remember "P", you are my boy and I got your back." Garrett exclaimed.

"Thanks a lot. That means a lot coming from you. Besides, the military offered me a hefty enlistment bonus-a big number."

"What's a big number because I know you?" as Garrett turned his head.

"50K," Pearson responded. "Damn, that is a big number," as Garrett's jaw dropped. "That is more than some people make in an entire year."

"I know. It's not so much the money but it helps. With the sale of the tutoring business and my enlistment bonus, I can give mom some money to buy herself something nice. She's always been putting us ahead of everyone and everything."

"You are right. Ms. Betty always had a good word to share. She definitely made sure you guys had what you needed. Besides, I like your mom's cooking," as the two friends laughed.

* * *

After Officer Training School, Pearson arrived at the Cyber Operations and Intelligence School for his advanced training. He sat in a classroom with about nine other students. As they talked among themselves, everyone wondered what was in store. Moments later, a thin well-groomed man with glasses came into the room wearing civilian clothes. He sat on the table without saying a word. All the students looked at each other but no one said anything. After about ten minutes, one of the candidates broke the silence.

"Are you the instructor?" he said.

The thin man didn't utter a word.

"Are you the instructor?" he asked again as he mumbled something to himself.

"Yes, I am your instructor and you have already failed the first test," replied the thin man.

The man introduced himself to the class and

provided an overview. He told the students that only about half of the nine remaining students would successfully complete the courses. "Based on the course's rigorous demands and work load, some of you won't make it to graduation." Pearson told himself that he could endure anything. He had faced challenges; therefore, failure wasn't an option.

After he completed his six months of training, Pearson was working in the cyber operations field. He rarely wore his military uniform and wasn't required to be clean shaven according to normal military standards. With hair over his ears and wearing a goatee, he looked more like a "hippie" than a military officer. His areas of expertise were biometric identification, authentication, and data storage. While working on a special project for rapid identification using biometrics, Pearson saw a business opportunity. Unfortunately, he was unable to pursue the venture due to the military's conflict of interest policy, which prohibited any outside employment potentially conflicting with military operations. After completing his seven-year obligation, Pearson left the service with an extensive knowledge of biometrics and artificial intelligence.

* * *

Pearson transitioned out of the military with ease and moved to Chicago, IL. Based on his nontraditional role in the Army, he adapted seamlessly with no major lifestyle adjustments required. He had saved most of his money in anticipation of starting his tech company. Always industrious, he invested most of his money from the sale of his tutoring company years earlier. With his skills, assertiveness, and background, Pearson had multiple job opportunities. However, he wasn't interested in working for a large corporation.

Pearson took some time to figure out his next move. In the meantime, he began lining up venture capital funding for his startup. He started with local resources in Chicago. Most of the Venture Capitalist (VC) s in the area was concentrated in the medical field. With his extensive knowledge in biometrics and data storage, he created an enterprising idea. While reading an article about hospital management, Pearson discovered a big opportunity for patient record management. He wrote the business plan to use biometrics to revolutionize the way hospitals admit patients, access patients' records, and execute medical billing. After extensive research, Pearson identified an innovative method to meet Health Insurance and Portability Accountability Act (HIPAA) privacy requirements and reduce admission time and medical billing administrative cost by 63 percent, which he quickly patented.

Through a mutual associate, Pearson met Jonathan Westin. Jonathan was intelligent, savvy, and extremely connected. He had been in the venture capitalism business for over 10 years. He graduated from Tinsel University in Aurora, IL where he studied Biology. He initially wanted to be a physician but took an interest in business after 3 years toward earning his degree. He got a job at a brokerage firm as an analyst through a relative referral. He quickly learned the business and eventually completed his graduate degree from Harvard. Jonathan always had an entrepreneurial spirit, which led him into venture capitalism. Throughout his distinguished career, he obtained funding for 23 businesses; and took seven of those startups public with a total portfolio of over $4.3 billion.

Although divorced, Jon was popular with women. His voice was soft and raspy—conveying a soothing spirit. He was warm, mysterious and charming. Jonathan stood 6'2" tall with dark hair with touches of gray along the temples. His statue and presence often own the room upon entry. His piercing blue eyes had a way of looking through a woman's soul mesmerizing her with each spoken word. His conversations were often brief, pointed but not choppy. He chose every word carefully. Jon liked a sassy, smart but grounded woman. He despised a passive-spirited personality especially when it came to women. In other words, Jon liked the "hunt" when it came to women. He had claimed many "trophies" throughout the years but was always looking for his next conquest.

Jon also enjoyed the nightlife. He often visited major upscale private clubs in the Chicago area. In his social circles, money was no object when it came to entertainment. The best of spirits and wines, private chefs, and French cuisine were the rules not the exceptions. Jon worked hard to gain his prestigious position and he enjoyed the "fruits of his labor."

The two men met in a quite restaurant one autumn afternoon to discuss the possibilities of a joint venture. After the normal pleasantries, they got down to business.

"Tom tells me you are looking to grow a startup business incorporating biometrics for hospital identification and medical records management. Can you tell me a little bit more about your idea?"

"Sure—It's a revolutionary approach to record access management. The concept involves the use of biometrics to identify patient's records using a two-factor authentication (something you are and something you know). Once the patients are identified and authenticated, an Artificial Intelligence (AI) server will use the information to access all records. In essence, the entire person's medical history can be accessible by the AI server by data mining information from various databases and consolidating this information to a mobile device. The AI server meets HIPAA and other security requirements." Pearson spoke confidently.

"Pearson that sounds good but have there has been any practical applications of this AI server system interface. What about government approval for this technology?" Jon sharply retorted.

"I know there is a lot of discussion in Washington about AI technology and how this technology walks a 'fine line' when it comes to patient privacy. I know there is active legislation to curb AI development." Jon replied." Also, I've seen several claims of AI usage but the majority of the systems were just glorified databases that didn't provide any real value."

"I don't see any governmental issues with my

technology. There are safeguards in place to mitigate the risks associated with data loss. In addition, I will be glad to show you my designs and prototypes if that will ease your uncertainty. I have already gotten the first series of funding necessary to begin the testing. I'm asking you to fund my venture in exchange for 40 percent in equity with a stock option buyback in three years when we take the company public."

"That's a bold and ambitious statement. I've heard that before from a lot of entrepreneurs," as Jon sat back in his chair.

"Perhaps you have but you haven't heard it from me," as Pearson looked Jon directly in the eye.

"I like you confidence and assertiveness. Let's see where this adventure takes us," Jonathan replied.

The two men had a deal. This was the start of their long-term partnership.

* * *

[Meetings in Washington DC convene for the Patient and Privacy Act. This proposed bill will allow the use of Artificial Intelligence technology usage in an effort to reduce costs within the health care industry.]

"Congressman Pennington, I'm not sure what your position is toward the Artificial Intelligence research but we would like your support and endorsement for the bill. We feel the legislation will be very beneficial for the health care industry, specifically hospitals," replied Mr. Covington, Chairman of the AI lobbying group.

"I'm not in favor of that particular bill. I believe this proposal directly conflicts with Health Insurance

Portability and Accountability Act (HIPAA). Authorizing and allowing a server the ability to access information across multiple databases that don't have a "need to know" is preposterous. This fact negates individual privacy. Who is to say this information won't end up in the wrong hands or sold on the 'black market?' With recent breaches of information at major retailers and banks, this is just another opportunity for adversaries to gain access to sensitive information." The Congressman replied.

"Besides, I've heard rumors that data storage companies sell Personal Identifiable Information (PII) to pharmaceutical companies for marketing purposes. The drug companies target individuals and hospitals based on patient profiling to better tailor their marketing efforts. Pharmaceutical companies will have 'insider' information about medicines patients are taking. Furthermore, these same companies may exploit the data through trend analysis to reveal medicines hospitals prescribe; amounts supplied; and the economies of scale for distribution."

"Congressman, we assure you that the information retrieved will only be used for the intended purpose which is to better manage patients' records. Personal information will not be shared with a third party. We aren't sure of your information sources and the reliability of data," responded Mr. Covington.

"I'm going to have to do some additional research before I can endorse this bill. We will reschedule our next review in 30 days." Meeting adjourned.

"We need something on the Congressman. I realize he is the chairperson for the sub-committee but we need something to sway his vote and influence our way," coldly retorted the Chairman of the Artificial Intelligence lobbying group. "We represent some of the most powerful corporations in the world. We have to turn this guy. Does he have any issues with any family, vices, or dependencies? Does he have a mistress? I want you guys to dig into his life and find me some dirt."

Sir, he has a daughter that lives in Chicago. She is going through a divorce and a nasty custody battle," the associate eagerly announced.

"Anything we can do to smear the Congressman's name. We can characterize him as a terrible father through scandal and bad publicity. We can use this information as leverage. I need something," replied Mr. Covington.

* * *

Over the next three years, Pearson and Jonathan worked feverously to grow the business. Pearson worked on building the brand by targeting major hospitals and medical centers in the greater Chicago area with expansion plans throughout the Midwest. He continued to solicit business through direct marketing, associations, and other avenues to reach prospective clients. It wasn't long before the business began to gain traction. Mount Sinai General Hospital was his first major account. At the time, the organization had 25 hospitals across three states.

Pearson signed on one hospital after another building his business brand. Soon, Jon and Pearson were preparing to launch the Initial Public Offering (IPO) for PC Westin Services, Inc.

The IPO was a huge success. Many friends, family and business associates called to congratulate Pearson on his success. His hard work had finally paid off. He was a successful businessman.

He flew home to visit his mother. It had been months since his last visit. He knocked on the door.

"Mom, I'm home," he spoke.

She opened the door and greeted him with open arms and a kiss on the cheek.

"When did you get into town?"

"I just got in and I came by to see you because I have a surprise for you."

"What did you do? Did you get married? Are you giving me a grandchild?"

"No mom," Pearson replied. "I do have keys for you."

"Keys?" She replied.

"Yes, I have keys for you." Pearson spoke.

Pearson and his mother drove to a modern house at the end of a street in a nice subdivision.

He opened the door and handed her the keys.

"Remember back when I was thirteen? I told you I would become a successful businessman and take you away from all your struggling and misfortune. Well, my company just went public and I'm doing well enough to buy you a new house. I know how much you sacrificed for us so I wanted to do something nice for you."

At this point, his mother had tears in her eyes. She broke down and hugged him. She couldn't believe he remembered and kept his promise. They laughed, talked and caught up on family matters. Pearson stayed in town for a few days before his departure back to Chicago.

* * *

Pearson continued building his business as the CEO, with expanded operations extending to the West Coast. His executive team recommended he attend a big hospital conference scheduled in the coming months in Los Angeles. At first, he was reluctant to attend. However, after speaking with other colleagues, he was convinced the conference would be an excellent opportunity to network and build relationships in the West Coast market. Jonathan agreed the conference would be a good opportunity to network and explore new business ventures. Jon flew out a couple days early on his private jet. Pearson would have accompanied him on his flight but he had a few loose ends to tie up before the four-day conference.

Major hospitals had booths to promote their products and services. Hospital administrators and other executives were participating in a variety of seminars and workshops. Jon arrived at the main conference floor and walked around to get a "feel" for the organizations attending. Across the main hall stood a tall curvy woman with her back turned. Jon liked the view and wanted to get a closer look. As he walked toward her, she turned around. Jon smiled to himself as he thought that the view from the front was even better than he imagined.

Always well groomed in tailored suits and custom shoes, Jon had impeccable taste when it came to clothes. Jonathan smiled as he met Julie. She was polite and courteous. However, she didn't appear receptive to his normally charming persona. She projected a polite but uninterested vibe as she bid him farewell. Jon was surprised. He was accustomed to getting what he wanted. However, Julie was atypical. For whatever reason, Julie looked familiar to him but he couldn't ascertain the context. Perhaps, since he had met so many people throughout his career, he wasn't sure if she knew her at all.

* * *

Julie Pennington was the only daughter to John Pennington, a prominent Congressman from Portland, Maine. Julie had two older brothers. As the only girl growing up in a house with two brothers, she learned to be assertive when necessary but always maintaining her feminine posture. Her father gave his "baby girl" the love she needed to grow and become a sophisticated woman. Her mother was the well-respected Director of Nursing in the largest hospital in Portland. Between her parents and brothers, her family loved, cared for, and appreciated Julie. Her brothers were very protective of their little sister when she was growing up, which made dating for her awkward.

Julie excelled in academics. Although her mother wanted her to "follow in her footsteps" and become a nurse, Julie was not interested in nursing at all. She was more interested in business. She enjoyed the medical field but wasn't interested in all the nuisances of caring for patients; that was her mother's life work. Upon completion of high school, Julie had an opportunity to attend any of the top schools in the country. Although a few Ivy League schools accepted her, she chose a little school on the outskirts of Chicago. She picked Tinsel University. Her parents believed she was rebelling against their wishes by picking an unknown school in the Midwest. Actually, she picked a small school in a quiet environment where she could have a normal college experience without the pressure and media attention connected with being the daughter of a prominent Congressman. Perhaps, she chose an unknown school as a way to get from under the protective arms of her brothers. She wanted to grow but felt she couldn't do that with her brothers serving such a protective role.

Julie enjoyed college like any other young adult away from home. Although she was initially homesick being so far away, she used the distance as a way to mature. Julie was active in social organizations, participated in various rallies of interest, but primarily focused on her academics. She dated a few guys in college but no one serious. Her sexual experience was limited to only a couple of guys. She did date one guy her senior year but she ended the relationship because she wasn't ready for anything serious.

After graduation, Julie got a job at a local hospital in Chicago. After a couple of years, she went back to graduate school and earned her master's degree in Health Administration. She met her future husband, and they were eventually married a couple years later. Julie Pennington married Thomas Barber, a prominent merger and acquisition attorney in the area. Thomas was seven years her senior. Things went well between Julie and her husband. They welcomed their only son a year into their marriage. Both parents had hectic schedules with Thomas's job requiring frequent travel. Julie carried the brunt of the parenting responsibilities as she juggled conflicting priorities as a working mother.

After six years of marriage, things began to break down. Julie felt Thomas wasn't living up to his obligation as a father. His work required him to travel frequently. She often felt overburdened and overwhelmed with working and parenting while her husband missed most of the parental challenges. Her thoughts turned from frustration to resentment because Thomas wasn't empathetic to her feelings. She had a career as well. She was committed to being a mother. However, she didn't want to be a single parent.

"Honey, I'm home. It's been a very busy week for me. Negotiations broke down on the Harris Corporation deal. I ended up working 12 hours almost every night this week. I'm exhausted. What's been going on here? How is Johnny?" as he gives her an emotionless kiss on the cheek on his way to the sofa.

"I haven't watched TV this week. It's been so

hectic. What did you cook?" he mumbled as he flipped through the channels.

"You hardly called this week. How dare you come in here and ask what's going on as if we are roommates. I can't believe your condescending attitude. You don't have a damn clue what the hell is going on here and it looks like you don't even care." She yelled.

"This is the same story every damn week. You come in here as if you have conquered the world and you are the only one with a demanding job. I have a demanding career as well and I still have to be mommy because you've been absent as a parent." She yelled.

"You are being unreasonable and selfish. We are both parents. We just have different roles. I am involved. Even though I'm not here every day, doesn't mean I'm not involved." Thomas replied in a condescending tone.

Julie stormed out of the room and slammed the door.

Finally, after years of marriage, Julie filed for divorce. She sought joint custody with her as the custodian parent of their 7-year-old son. Thomas strongly disagreed and felt his son should be with his father. The custody battled enraged and quickly degraded to toxic recriminations. Several divorce attorneys were involved with both parties going back and forth with no immediate concessions. Neither side was willing to compromise.

Because her personal life was in shambles, Julie focused on her work. Recently promoted to hospital administrator the previous year, things were going well for her professionally. She made significant strides as an administrator looking for ways to cut costs and improve operational efficiencies. One of her professional colleagues mentioned to her about an upcoming major hospital conference in Los Angeles. She needed to get away so this would be a perfect opportunity.

Julie's time at the conference was productive. She met some interesting professionals and expanded her network. During one of the social functions, she met a couple other women administrators. Overall, the conference turned out to be an excellence get-a-way and networking opportunity.

On the final day of the conference, Pearson spoke with many organizations with booths. His focus was to make contact for potential business opportunities. As he was leaving, he spotted Julie going through another exit. She caught his eye on a personal level. As a prudent businessman, he rarely considered personal involvement in a business setting but Julie was different. He wanted to meet her but missed the opportunity. Perhaps, he thought, it wasn't meant to be.

As he was boarding his flight back to Chicago the next morning, he checked his boarding pass to locate his seat. Coincidentally, Julie boarded the same flight. He felt he was lucky but not this lucky. She sat on the row ahead of him with a vacant seat on the other side of her. As passengers boarded and found their respective seats, Pearson wondered if anyone would sit next to her. Just as the flight attendant was making final preparations to close the door, an elderly lady arrived and took her seat next to Julie. The woman saw Pearson's disappointment as the two of them made eye contact. She asked if Pearson could help stow her overhead bag. Pearson was gracious and receptive to assist.

"Young man, I like a window seat. "Would you mind switching seats with me?" she winked.

"No Ma'am. I wouldn't mind at all," Pearson gladly replied.

Pearson had gotten an excellent opportunity courtesy of the elderly woman in first class. Julie partially noticed the exchange as she casually browsed through her brochures from the conference. Within this small window of opportunity, Pearson caught her eye. With her personal life in chaos, she found it difficult to imagine starting over or even considering anything or anyone but this guy was different. His vibe was good and positive. Besides, he had helped the elderly woman with her bag and switched seats with her. This led her to believe he was at least courteous and respectable.

"Hello, how are you?" Pearson calmly spoke.

"I'm doing well." Julie replied in a warm and friendly voice.

"Do you fly a lot?" Pearson asked.

"No, this is the first time I have flown in a while. I don't fly much because of work."

"I noticed you were looking at brochures from the conference in LA. Did you attend?"

"Yes."

"Really I did too."

"Are you an administrator as well?"

"No I provide professional services to hospitals."

"I apologize, my mother raised me better. I'm Pearson Caldwell."

"I'm Julie Barber. Please to meet you," As she shook his hand and made eye contact. Julie noticed Pearson's light brown eyes and exceptional smile.

Pearson noticed Julie's soft rosy lips, almond colored skin, and natural auburn colored hair. The two of them noticed each other—both trying hard to avoid the obvious.

"What did you think about the conference?"

"I thought it was good. I attended a few of the seminars and social events. I met a couple other women administrators as well."

"What brought you to the conference?" Julie asked.

"Mainly, it was a plane similar to this one and then a taxi." Pearson replied with quick wit and an expressionless face.

Julie laughed. "That was a good one. You got with that one."

"I provide professional IT services to help hospitals and businesses manage patient admission, medical billing, and data storage services at significant cost savings."

"That's interesting. Managing medical billing and record management are two of my most challenging areas. I would like to learn more."

"I would be happy to set up a meeting to show you

what my company does and if we can mutually benefit from a professional relationship."

"That sounds good," the two of them exchanged business cards.

A couple of days later, Pearson followed up with a phone call saying how pleased he was to have met her and how he wanted to get on her calendar to discuss the benefits his company's services provide. Pearson really wanted to see her again on a personal level but didn't want to send the wrong message and sound inappropriate. If she was married and saw the communication as only a business relationship, mentioning anything other than business related topics could be perceived as unprofessional. He had to walk a 'fine line' between personal intentions and projecting the right professional image

Julie was sorting through her thoughts as well. Her imagination was out of control as she processed so many emotions. Thomas had already moved out of the house over a year ago. The two of them shared custody of their 7-year-old son. She didn't want a divorce but she couldn't continue her life with Thomas. In her opinion, he was just too selfish and her life with him was all but finished. Soon she would be able to put her life back together. In this midst of all this emotional turbulence, her thoughts were on a new man. Julie was interested in Pearson but didn't want to send the wrong impression. Although she felt they had good chemistry on the plane as they chatted, perhaps he wasn't interested in her on a personal level.

Finally, Pearson exercised boldness and asked her out to lunch to discuss a business opportunity. He took a big risk by asking her out even if she wasn't interested in his company's professional services. What did he have to lose at this point?

"Julie, it's nice to see you again." Pearson said as they shook hands.

Yes, it has been a while. My schedule has been so hectic since I returned from the conference. It happens every time I leave the office on travel."

"I do understand. I appreciate you taking the time to at least hear my presentation. I promise to be brief and cover the key points."

Pearson presented his company services, features, and benefits. She was impressed with his articulate presentation skills but she was daydreaming of intimate times with Pearson. From holding hands to walks in the park, her intimate passionate thoughts were wondering uncontrollably throughout her mind and imagination. Her mind was creating scenes for an on-going fascination of hopeful thoughts to personify and come to fruition.

Julie said she would review the information and present it to the hospital board. If they approved, the hospital would like an implementation plan with timelines. She said she'd be in touch and would give him a call soon.

A week later, Julie called Pearson to let him know the hospital wasn't interested in pursuing an IT system upgrade at this time. He understood and thanked her for the follow-up call. Although disappointed, Pearson was somewhat relieved because he really wanted to know Julie on a personal level and by having a business relationship with the hospital, this may raise questions of a conflict of interest.

Two weeks later, Pearson called Julie on a Thursday.

"Hello, Julie?"

"Yes?"

"This is Pearson Caldwell from the plane trip from LA. I presented some information about an IT system."

"I remember you. How are you? How are things going?"

"Things are going well. I'm keeping busy with my business. I am sure you are probably wondering why I'm calling."

"Yes, I didn't expect your call," As she smiled.

"I know this may seem awkward but life is too short. Would you go to dinner with me?"

Julie paused and hesitated before answering. So many thoughts raced through her mind in that instance. She knew she couldn't wait too long to respond in fear of rejecting him. She wasn't sure if she was ready to date again. Her divorce wasn't final but it had been over a year since Thomas moved out and it was time to begin living again and moving on with her life.

"What day were you thinking," She asked apprehensively. It wasn't as if she had a busy social calendar. She had become engrossed in her work as a coping mechanism for her unstable personal life.

"I was thinking Saturday Night around 7pm. I can

pick you around 6:30pm and we can head to dinner from there. You can text your address. Do you like jazz music?"

"Yes, I do."

"Sounds good. Here is my cell number. Feel free to give me a call if you have any questions or if anything comes up."

"Ok. I will talk to you soon."

"Bye."

"Bye."

Julie was distracted for the rest of the afternoon. She didn't know what to think of Pearson. He seemed nice but she wasn't sure. She overanalyzed every thought, scenario, and instance thinking of the most bizarre possibilities imaginable. Julie's thoughts were out of control. She called her friend Sarah to help her sort through all the possibilities.

"I'm so overwhelmed at this point. I don't know what to do. I haven't been this nervous about a man since my first time in college. I don't know what to wear. I don't want to dress like an old lady. However, I don't want to dress like a tramp either. I'm losing it. Maybe I should just cancel the date. I'm not ready."

"Julie, Julie, Julie. Take a deep breath." Sarah said as she sat down with her.

"It's only a first date. It's not the CPA exam. You are going to be fine. You just have to relax. Based on what you have told me, he seems like a really nice guy."

"You're probably right. I do need to relax about this situation. Sarah, he is hot."

"Oh really?" Sarah replied with surprise.

"Oh my God! He is tall (at least over 6 feet), strong arms, broad shoulders, slender waist with a nice round butt. He could throw me around anytime. Oops. Did I say that aloud? I know I shouldn't be thinking those sorts of thoughts. It's been a long time and you know a girl has needs."

Julie sighed and Sarah laughed. It was hard to tell who was getting more excited: Julie or Sarah.

* * *

Pearson arrived at exactly 6:30pm. Perhaps his military training and background caused him to exercise such a high degree of promptness. He rang the doorbell to her rustic brownstone located in a quiet suburban neighborhood.

"I will be right down." Julie replied over the intercom.

She looked out the window to see what Pearson drove but more specifically, what he was wearing. He was well groomed in a tailored dark blue jacket, champagne colored shirt, and dark blue slacks with brown loafers to match. Pearson waited patiently as Julie made her way to the bottom of the stairs. His eyes lit up when he saw her. With her hair up, she was wearing a sleek black sleeveless dress, a string of pearls, and a touch of makeup with a neutral shade of lipstick. She casually but gracefully stepped out in her 2" pomp's as if she was gliding on air. He opened the door for her and soon they were on their way.

"You look very nice tonight; but you look nice every time I see you."

"Thank you Pearson."

The two talked on their way to the restaurant. After valet parking, the two of them walked into *Charlie's*.

The host greeted the couple and quickly seated them near the front of the stage. There was smooth piano music playing; several muted conversations served to stimulate the ambiance. The low lighting complimented the exquisite wine and delectable food. The sights, the sounds, and the smells had created a picture of entertainment.

"I have never been here before. It has a unique atmosphere."

"I'm glad you like it. That is why I asked you if you liked Jazz. The place has a cozy relaxed feeling."

"I agree." Julie responded.

The couple spent time over dinner talking, getting to know each other. Both kept the conversation light. It was the first date and first dates are sometimes tricky.

Pearson walked Julie to her door.

"I had a really nice time."

"I did as well."

"I look forward to speaking with you and seeing you again." Pearson replied as he gazed into her eyes.

"I would like that."

At that moment, he leaned over to give her a gentle embrace as he kissed her on the cheek.

"Give me a call when you get in."

"Definitely, I will talk to you soon."

The phone rang mid-morning. Julie answered. "Hey Sarah, What's going on?"

"How was your date? You know I want all the details."

"A lady never kisses and tells." Julie replied in a facetious sophisticated tone.

"Girl, I'm only kidding. It was amazing. We went to this restaurant called *Charlie's*. They had a very good band, excellent service, and the food was wonderful. I had a really great time."

"So will you see him again?"

"Yes, he is a total gentleman and he has a body. Oh My!" The two friends laughed as Julie shared the details of the date. This was the first time she had been on a date since the separation and the first time in years, she had been out with a man other than her husband. She was chartering new territory. It was scary, unfamiliar but exciting.

Over the following weeks, the two of them went on several dates. After dinner one evening, they decided to go for a walk along the water.

"Pearson, I have something I want to talk to you about."

"What is it? Are you a man? Are you leaving the planet?"

"I'm serious."

"I'm sorry. What is it?"

"I'm still technically married. I filed for divorce but it's not final yet. My soon-to-be ex and I are involved in a nasty custody battle over our son. I know I should have told you earlier but I didn't want to seem like I was bringing a lot baggage to the situation."

"I kind of figured something was going on that you weren't telling me. I figured you would share when you felt comfortable. I learned a long time ago not to pressure anyone for anything. Eventually, that person will share. If not, then I will excuse myself from the situation."

"I feel so bad for not telling you on the first date but that would have been awkward." She replied as she turned away.

"The important thing is that you told me. Don't keep things from me, ok?"

"I won't."

Pearson pulled her close and gave her a kiss. His lips pressed against her soft luscious lips, tasting like sweet strawberries dipped in warm chocolate. He had been yearning to taste those lips since the first time he met her months ago. Pearson played these thoughts in his head as his mind wondered.

Julie was so excited. She felt a different level of exhilaration. Pearson had broken into her imagination, connected with her inner thoughts and made passionate love to her inner sensuality. In her mind, he was whispering his words in her ear until it sounded like her mind's voice was urging her to bring her sensual thoughts to fruition. She could feel his strong but gentle hands rubbing all over her body in the love scene of her mind's movie. She couldn't wait to see him again.

The following weekend, Pearson and Julie went

dancing on Friday Night. He really enjoyed spending time with her. She was an excellent dancer. She always wanted to go dancing with Thomas but he wasn't interested in dancing or the nightlife.

On Saturday night, the couple went back to *Charlie's*. One of Julie's favorite singers was in town for a special show. Pearson surprised her with tickets. He thought it would be a nice gesture.

It was a special and amazing night for her. She was at one of her favorite restaurants; spending special times with a delightful man while enjoying live entertainment. The show continued as she turned the mental page. The lights went down as all eyes shifted to center stage. The artist was singing all of her favorite songs. The music selection was a blend of old and new creating an appreciation for the new while the old songs created a feeling of déjà vu.

Still early, the two arrived at Julie's house. Pearson walked her to the door as he had done so many times before.

"I had a wonderful time as always Julie."

"It doesn't have to end now. Would you like to come in for a night cap?"

Surprised, Pearson said. "Yes."

She led him into her brownstone as she asked him his beverage of choice. He chose brandy and the two of them continue their conversation. He was looking at her, she was looking at him, and they both were looking at the situation. He walked over to toast to a wonderful evening. When she approached him, he pulled her close to taste her sweet lips and to feel her curvaceous body against him. He turned her around so he could gently massage her arms and shoulders as he whispered in her ear. "Do you feel my strong but gentle hands rubbing all over your body in the love scene of your mind's movie? If you do, then you will know my hands are going up and down your back running my fingers through your hair as I pull you close to kiss your sensuous lips above and below your navel.

I want you to feel me breathing on the back of your neck as my arms embrace you with a warm hug that shows you that I want to take this situation to the next level. I know this is an evolution and escalation of the situation."

Pearson's hands were constantly on her smooth golden skin exploring the contours of her womanly features. From her twin peaks forming a ridge, to the flatlands—down her treasure trail to the edge of her tavern of passion, he experienced them all. As he kissed her deeply and passionately, her body was on fire. Her fire was a flame that burned but didn't go out.

He licked the back of her neck as he breathed in her ear and on her skin caressing her twin peaks as two delicate mounds of excitement. He rubbed along the inside of her thigh starting at the top of her knee going upward to the edge of her wetness. She moaned in anticipation of him touching her hot wet spot. He asked her was her special place throbbing as she turned around to grab his butt while pulling him close so she could feel his hardness. At that moment, she led him upstairs to her bedroom. When she reached the top of the stair, he pushed her on the bed. He sucked her fingers one by one swirling his tongue around each one as he looked into her eyes. Pearson sucked on her neck, and unbuttoned her blouse and bra to expose her tender nipples. He covered them with his hot mouth; swirling his soft wet tongue around the tips as he pushed them in and out. He sucked on her nipples, gently biting them as she moaned with excitement. With his strong hands, he squeezed her tips as his tongue went back and forth to taste then like his favorite ice cream cone.

Julie's breathing became short and irregular as Pearson kissed her more passionately. His tongue teased her hot wet mouth as she sucked on his lower lip. He stretched her arms over her head as he licked under her chin and sucked on her earlobes. With her face in his strong hands, he ran his fingers through her hair gently tugging as he licked her lips. She arched her back as her body begged for more. He was between her legs pressing and grinding against her softness. She wanted him. She could feel it. His hardness made her special spot throb and drip with her natural juices of wetness. She had never had a man between her legs that ignited this level of heat and intensity.

She quickly unbuttoned his pants and slid him inside of her wet pond of passion. He could feel her juicy tightness as she received all of him inside. He teased her by taking his stiffness out. She gasped as if someone had suddenly stolen her breath. She begged him to put his hard rod of pleasure back inside. She arched her back as her body begged without saying a word. Her legs were locked around him with his key deep inside her your treasure box.

The deeper he went, the more she whimpered. She moaned like a puppy, as he showed no mercy punishing her delicate kitten. Her nails dug deep into his back attempting to claw her way out of the situation or was she subconsciously inviting me to go deeper. He could feel her tension building. She was cuming, as he pumped faster, deeper and harder inside until they both released the orgasmic beast of intensity! Both had reached that erotic crescendo. The couple collapsed into a satisfying slumber of release; cuddling as they both drifted off into the afterglow of excitement and relaxation.

The next morning, Julie rolled over to discover Pearson was missing from her bed. She suddenly had an empty abandonment feeling until the aroma of eggs, bacon and toast teased her nose. She ventured downstairs to a stronger smell of food. Pearson had prepared breakfast. She was so surprised she didn't know what to say.

"Oh you didn't have to make breakfast."

"It's no big deal. I wanted to surprise you. You were sleeping so sound and peaceful. I'm an early riser so I thought I would take advantage of the time."

The two of them enjoyed a quiet morning of breakfast and conversations. Julie was constantly smiling as she shared moments with Pearson. He cherished his time with her.

* * *

Over the following weeks, Pearson and Julie enjoyed each other's time getting to know one another. She discovered how funny, playful, and outgoing he was. She also discovered he had a sensitive side when it came to his mother and his siblings. He didn't speak much about his dad and she didn't push him to do so.

Pearson learned more about Julie as well. He learned more about her life, family, and background. She had grown up in a sheltered environment. She had a limited perspective of the regular challenges of life: poverty, divorce, and conflict. Her parents were still married after more than 40 years. She was struggling with the pending divorce and custody battle. Although she would be relieved to move forward with her life, she didn't envision getting a divorce because her parents were still married despite the vicissitudes that came with being together so long.

Work demands heated up for both of them but that didn't stop them from seeing one another when their schedules permitted. Pearson called or texted her with encouraging messages. He understood the pressures of juggling a career when one's personal life is in chaos.

"Hello."

"How is my sexy hospital administrator today? Are you conquering the world as usual?"

Julie sighed and smiled. "You know just when to call don't you?"

"I figured you were buried under work and I thought I would be your verbal archeologist."

She smiled and twirled her hair like a schoolgirl.

"How is your day?"

"It's going well. I'm adding new accounts on a weekly basis. The software has really improved operations for several hospitals so my clients are happy—and so are my shareholders."

"I called to check on you for two reasons: because you were in my thoughts; and I wanted to hear your voice."

Julie smiled and blushed. "I bet you say that to all the girls?"

"I only say those things to the special girl in my life."

She had a warm feeling come over her body as her imagination ran wild. Pearson had awakened a passionate beast. He had a way of distracting her by sending her thoughts down a naughty and sensual trail. With Pearson as her "captain," he commanded her "man in the boat" like Columbus commanded the Piñata, Niña, and Santa Marina taking her sexuality to unchartered territory.

"What city are you in this week?"

"Denver. You should come out to visit me. I'm stuck in town over the weekend. We are doing a major system implementation."

"That sounds so tempting. I bet the weather is great."

"It is. All you have to do is say yes and I will make the arrangements."

She paused. She thought of a bunch of reasons why

she shouldn't just drop everything and fly out Friday evening.

"I've always wanted to visit Denver in the summer."

"Then it's settled. I will email you the details. Wear something sexy that compliment your legs." Pearson replied as he laughed.

Julie was somewhat distracted for the remainder of the afternoon. Friday finally arrived. She had been anticipating her trip since Tuesday. Although she hadn't seen Pearson in a week, it seemed like forever. Her body was yearning for his strong but gentle touch. She longed to be held-feeling that sense of security in his arms. She boarded the plane by mid-afternoon on her way to Denver. Pearson was at the airport when her flight arrived. He had gotten her a single red rose. He was so excited to see her. With her hair in a ponytail, she had on a loosely fitting blouse, a short mini skirt and sandals. He wanted to take her right there at the airport. The chemistry between the two of them was unprecedented.

Her flight's arrival gate was in an older section of the airport. Because of the airport expansion, older terminals were under major construction. It was a long walk from the arrival gate to the main corridor. Most passengers took the shuttle to the main terminal but Pearson figured they could walk and talk on their way to the car.

He gave her a big warm hug and caressed her as he kissed her on the cheek. She whispered in his ear.

"Before you ask, I have on black lace panties."

Pearson was speechless. He hadn't seen this side of her. As they walked down the long corridor toward the main terminal, he stopped by the restroom. He went inside and surveyed to see if anyone else was present. He came out as he looked both ways and pulled her inside immediately locking the door. Neither of them thought much about getting caught, but of the thrilling adventure. After all, the area was remotely located from the main terminal and there weren't any other flights scheduled to arrive in this section of the terminal, so the risk of being discovered was low.

Behind that locked door, the two of them became one. There wasn't much talking only touching. They were like animals showing their animalistic instincts. Pearson raised her skirt as he grabbed two handfuls of her round cheeks. Deep passionate kisses continued as her juices began to run down her thighs. He picked her up and put her on the sink. He stuck his finger inside her natural jar of honey to taste her juices as he licked his fingers. He yanked her lace thong to the side ripping the delicate fabric. After ripping her lace mask covering her treasure, he ran through her niceness like a sexual villain. She was the beauty and he was the beast. She wrapped her arms around his neck as he went deep inside; deep, hard and fast; in and out thrusting deeper each time. She moaned louder with each of his hard manly thrusts.

He turned her around and raised her skirt as she leaned over the sink. Once back inside, he grabbed and pulled a big handful of hair. Every time he pulled her hair, she moaned as he drove her hard like his racecar; giving her lots of throttle. He positioned his other large hand on her shoulder so she could feel his raw power as he pumped her hard, fast, and deep. She arched her back and breathed irregularly. He spanked her ass as he drove deep inside of her. He panted and growled while she whimpered like a new puppy in a new place.

They moved to a stall where she mounted him like the stallion he was. She grinded and pumped him as she rocked back and forth on top as he held on for the wild ride. Their eyes locked on each other as he pulled her back and forth deeper each time. He could see her erratic intense breathing as she gyrated vigorously.

The ride continued as she faced away but still rocking up and down on his hard rod. Pearson grabbed her shoulders, then her waist and eventually her thighs. She grinded her hips deeply and aggressively without regard for anything or anyone.

Suddenly, the two of then heard a tug on the door. Someone had tried to enter. Apparently, the person thought the restroom was closed due to construction. Julie and Pearson quickly dressed and prepared to leave. He looked outside the door as she stayed in the stall. It was all clear and they quickly exited the restroom as they made their way toward the car. They laughed aloud as they kissed.

"You are such a thrill seeker," Pearson said.

"Oh no, don't blame it all on me. It was your idea, remember?"

"I don't remember. The details are cloudy," as they laughed.

He dropped her off at his hotel; took a quick shower; and told her he would be back soon. Pearson checked on the status of the IT system implementation. Things were going well. He told his chief engineer to give him a call if there were any major issues.

Julie was re-living the excitement from earlier that day. She was reprocessing her thoughts and actions. Years ago, she would have never even imagined anything like that, let alone doing something so bold. Pearson helped her break down many of her inhibitions. She felt free, bold, and liberated. At this point, she realized she had led a sheltered life. She was embracing a new and uninhibited sexuality and she loved it.

Pearson arrived early evening as Julie was relaxing and enjoying a glass of wine. She had already planned to order room service but she wanted her dessert now. The episode from earlier in the day continued throughout the night.

Pearson arrived at the client site early. He wanted to get a fresh start and ensure things were going well and according to schedule. He was committed to seeing things through with major clients by being available and on-site.

Julie was checking her voicemail messages. She had received a message from her attorney asking her to return his call. She called him and he indicated there had been a new development in her custody case. He told her he would discuss the matter with her on

Monday when she returned. This news really put a damper on her get-a-way weekend. She decided she wasn't going to worry about something she couldn't affect over the weekend.

Pearson was able to leave the site and head back to the hotel with some daylight left. The two of them decided to explore the area. They saw the mountains, rolling hills and open areas. Julie thought it was beautiful and wanted to go skiing in season but didn't know how. They both decided they would learn together. Besides, it would be a good opportunity for him to spend time with his now "special lady."

* * *

Julie was back in the office on Monday. She called her attorney early afternoon to see what was going on. He told her that her soon-to-be ex-husband was demanding more visitation time; different terms for child support; and a lower alimony amount than earlier agreed. Negotiations over the previous weeks had become more and more brutal. Thomas was stubborn and accustomed to winning at all cost in most instances. The entire divorce was taking its toll on her emotionally and financially. She was exhausted from the anguish, frustration, and grief. Her frustration level was at its highest point. She felt Thomas was being spiteful because she asked for the divorce and he didn't want one. Things got so chaotic; Julie had to take a couple days off from work to deal with the emotional distress—she was mentally reduced to ruins. The only bright spot was Pearson. He was very understanding and allowed her the space she needed to work through this devastating ordeal. After a few weeks had passed, he wanted to see how she was holding up.

[Phone rings.]

"Hello?"

"How are you holding up baby doll?" Pearson spoke in his normal upbeat deep voice.

"Better now that I'm talking to you."

"Awe, I'm always here for you, baby. I wanted to give you some time to let you work through things."

"I miss you so much."

"I miss you too."

"When will I see you again?" as her voice sank.

"When would you like to see me?"

"Right now," she sighed.

"I'm on my way up."

"Really?"

"I will be there shortly."

Julie buzzed her assistant and told her to re-schedule the rest of her meetings slotted for the afternoon. Julie had a large spacious office up on the 37th floor of a plaza high rise. She loved the natural light. Often she would open the drapes to allow the brilliance and dominance of the sun's illumination and glow to warm her office. Autumn was approaching so she wanted to take advantage of the remaining sunny days. Her office building was located downtown overlooking the river flowing through the city. Luxury condominiums surrounded the downtown area commanding premium prices. It was the perfect place to live, work, and play if you could afford it.

Pearson did arrive shortly. Julie's assistant escorted him into the office.

"I'm so glad to see you" as she gave him a big hug. "How long have you been back in town?"

"I've been back only a couple of days. How are you really holding up these days? I know you have a lot going on but things will work out. They always do."

"You always have the right words to say and they are always encouraging." She replied.

"I got it from my mom. I grew up poverty-stricken and bitter but my mom was wealthy in spirit and often found ways to encourage us. I share those lessons with others as they go through life's challenges."

"I come bearing gifts."

"What did you bring?"

"Chocolate for the strawberries."

"Hmm. You do know how to work a girl," as she smiled.

Pearson had learned her well. He knew what she liked, how she liked things, etc. He began to feed her the chocolate dipped strawberries teasing her every time she tried to bit one.

"Why are you teasing me?"

"Because you like it!"

She smiled. "I will never tell."

He continued to tease her with the strawberries until his lips were close to hers. He enticed her by tantalizing her with his lips giving her small seductive kisses all over her face. She couldn't stand being taunted as she became more and more aroused.

"What are you doing to me?"

"All the things you like."

As she sat in her chair, he gestured for her to sit on top of her desk while he was on his knees. He took his finger stuck it in the chocolate and put it on her lips and into her mouth. She sucked his finger very erotically. He thought that was such a turn on. Her hands grabbed his face as if to kiss him but she licked his face instead. This sent chills up and down his back. He put his head under her skirt and licked up and down the inside of her thighs. He could feel her heat building as he yearned to taste her. He could smell her and he didn't mean her perfume. Her breathing shortened the higher he licked up her thigh. He could feel her wetness as his mouth breathed on her hot spot through her red lace panties. His tongue made small circles along the inside of her left thigh up to the edge of her tavern of passion down her other leg; he didn't miss a spot. He pulled her to the edge of her desk as his arms wrapped around her thighs. Finally, he tasted her womanly moisture for the very first time. His soft wet tongue was on the edge of her soft wet lips. He curled his tongue upward and inside to taste her juices as his finger explored her cave. His tongue went up and down, and round and round as he explored the contours of her womanhood. She arched her back and grabbed his head as she draped her legs over his shoulders. She moaned and breathed heavily as he flickered his tongue like an open flame flickers from a gentle breeze. The faster he licked, the more he mesmerized her as her tension grew.

"Don't stop!"

"Don't stop!"

"Baby, Don't stop!"

"Don't stop!" [There was a brief pause.]

"Oh, I'm cuming."

Julie covered her mouth to mask an incredible orgasmic scream. She exploded from pleasure as her thighs clinched uncontrollably around Pearson's head. Her eyes rolled back as he brought the thunder until it was summer rain flooding her passion pond with the juices of excitement and release. Her toes curled as she patted her feet to music that only she could hear.

Pearson had taken her places she hadn't gone, express emotions she couldn't show, and taught her things she didn't know. A few moments later, Pearson surfaced from underneath her skirt looking into her eyes to see an amazing level of release and satisfaction. She glistened from a glow of ecstasy.

"You are so bad."

"But it felt so good. That is probably why good girls love bad boys," As he licked his lips.

She was speechless. After drinking a couple bottles of water, she recovered and straightened her clothes to look presentable.

"Hopefully, you will have a relaxing afternoon," he said as he gathered his things to leave. He gave her a warm embrace and a soft kiss. He walked with swagger through the door leaving her with a smile on her face. Julie spent the remainder of the afternoon re-living all the pleasurable thoughts and events. She knew she couldn't focus on her work so she left the office early that day.

* * *

A week later, there was a manila envelope left at her front door. She was puzzled because she wasn't expecting anything. Perhaps Pearson had left her something as a way of surprising her. She opened the envelope to a horrifying discovery.

[*Julie,*

It looks like you are having a good time when you should be working. The man in the pictures doesn't look like your husband. There is a phone in the package. I will contact you at the appropriate time. I hope you aren't considering contacting the authorities or anyone else. If you are, don't be surprised if these pictures end up in the hands of your hospital Board of Directors or at your husband's law firm.]

Julie was devastated that she had put herself in such a precarious position. She experienced so many emotions from regret to anger. She had allowed an emotional moment, a moment of weakness to ruin all the things she had worked so hard to accomplish. She questioned her own judgment, values, and morals. How could she have made such a huge mistake? She then considered her son. If her actions were exposed, what would be the impact to her young son? So many questions raced through her mind.

Who would want to do something like this as she burst into tears? Was it Thomas? She knew he was stubborn and was willing to do anything to win this nasty custody battle. Was it someone she didn't know? Since her father was up for re-election, could it be someone that had a vendetta against him? What is this person's motivation? There were so many questions and she was fresh out answers.

Three days later, the phone from the package finally rang.

"Hello."

[The electronically distorted voice replied.]

"I see you can follow directions."

"Yes, what do you want with me?" Julie asked.

"I want you to entertain me. I like to watch. I want to see the good Congressman's daughter behave badly. I want to see you and your boyfriend get intimate. You have teased me with your rendezvous in your office. I want to see what you really can do."

"If I do this, will you stop all this and make this scandal go away?"

"Yes."

"How do I know if I can trust you to keep your word?"

"You don't," As the person disconnected the line.

Julie was so troubled. She didn't need this extra stress with all the other things going on. She felt trapped with this scandal looming over her head. Her time with Pearson was limited given her busy schedule, the upcoming divorce hearing, and now this disastrous situation.

The divorce battle was really heating up between the two attorneys. Thomas's lawyer continued to demand unrealistic custody terms. Neither side could come to a reasonable agreement leading to an inevitable long drawn out court hearing. This outcome would prove to be disastrous for Julie. She had a large hospital to manage; a child to raise; and a horrifying situation brewing on the horizon that could potential prove devastating for her custody case.

When Julie arrived home from work the next evening, there was another manila envelope at her door. She opened the envelope:

[October 11-12, 2014, Fleshing Vila Bed &Breakfast, Chatman Suite, Chicago, IL]

Later that evening, the phone from the previous package rang:

"Julie, it's time to entertain," spoke a distorted scrambled voice.

"I want this to end. Why are you torturing me? I have enough going on in my life."

"Yes, I'm aware of your pending divorce and custody issues."

"How do you know all this?"

"That's not important. What is important is that I get what I want and I always get what I want."

"What do you want me to do?"

"You and your lover will enjoy an evening at the

Bed & Breakfast. I will enjoy an evening of entertainment. I am the producer and you will be my leading lady. Make sure you bring your sexy lace unmentionables. I know how much women love lace against their skin."

"When does all of this end?"

"It ends when you follow all my instructions," the caller disconnected.

Julie didn't know what to do. She was torn between not showing up and following the caller's instructions in hopes of this nightmare ending. She weighed both options. Finally, she decided against her better judgment to go through with the ordeal. She thought, perhaps, this was all he wanted in a perverted kind of way. She couldn't figure out who was behind all of these messages.

* * *

Julie called Pearson.

"Hey baby. I'm sorry I've been distance these last few weeks. It's just been so overwhelming with my divorce and work. I am so stressed with all the things going on. I really need to get away even if it's only for a day. Can you make time for me next weekend?"

"I concluded you had a lot going on since I haven't heard from you. I knew you would reach out when the time was right. You know I haven't told you this lately but I really like you a lot and you're such an important part of my life. I can always make time you."

"Awe, don't make me cry. I miss you so much," with tears in her eyes.

"I miss you too."

"There is a Bed & Breakfast in North Chicago near Lincoln Park. I will text you the details."

"That sounds good. I will talk to you soon."

Everything was set. She felt bad not being able to be honest about why she picked that particular location. She remembered promising not to keep things from him. However, she knew the consequences of not sticking to the terms of the arrangement with her "blackmailer". She felt she didn't have a choice and she was out of time and options. When she called, the reservation was already on file under her name with all expenses paid.

The workweek leading up to the getaway was a blur. She had many work related issues, discussions with her attorney, and several parental responsibilities. At least she could look forward to seeing Pearson although the conditions weren't the most favorable. She resolved to get through all these chaotic events.

Julie picked up Pearson on the way to the B&B. The house was about 30 minutes from downtown Chicago overlooking Lake Michigan. It was October and the leaves had already begun to turn. Pearson loved the changing season. He felt autumn was that opportune moment for plants, shrubs, and trees to show their "true colors." Fall had set the stage and allowed each individual tree as well as a collection of trees, an opportunity to express their unique colorful personality and statue. Although these colorful expressions were limited like any theatrical performance, these expressions still left a lasting impression upon his mind until next fall arrived.

The B&B was in an exclusive well-established area near Lincoln Park. The Chatman Suite was exquisite. The house was a large 19th century detached brownstone with ornate brick designs complimenting huge archway and bay windows. The front entrance was an oversized 8' mahogany door with cast iron hinges. The suite was spacious with lots of windows allowing natural light in to baste the rooms during late autumn days.

"You made an excellent choice. I'm impressed," as Pearson strolled through the various rooms.

"There is even a patio with oversized lawn chairs off the main bedroom of this two bedroom retreat."

"Baby, look at this canopy bed. I always wanted a king size canopy bed," as she made romantic eye contact with Pearson.

"We're going to have a good time," as he grinned.

"You are so silly but I like it. You make me laugh."

After the two of them checked in and settled, they went for a ride to enjoy the fall weather. It was a sunny day and Pearson wanted to see all the different colors.

The sunroof was open as the breeze blew through Julie's hair. It was a cool autumn day with sun everywhere. Even with the sunroof open; he could still smell her perfume. The aroma was mixing with the cool fall air creating a combination that drew him closer to her. Her sundress did so many things for her curvaceous body as he appreciated each individual curve and contour hypnotizing him in unison as he drove down this winding road along the lake. He wanted to touch her but couldn't. His attraction to her was too strong for he knew her presence would consume his remaining self-control. His focus struggled to maintain direction as they rode on their way to no particular destination.

They stopped along the way to have a late lunch, site see, and enjoy the views. Clear skies or partially cloudy skies served as the background for the sunny autumn day producing strong desire to be outdoors. Cool breezy mornings, coupled with a favorite aromatic mocha, gave them a zestful appreciation of nature's gifts.

Day turned into evening as the two found a quiet little restaurant to enjoy a meal and conversation.

"As I was telling you on the phone, I really have enjoyed spending these last few months with you. I haven't taken much time to have a personal life or get involved with anyone but you turned my head without me looking. I almost didn't go to that conference but I'm so glad I did," Pearson spoke as he looked deeply into her eyes.

"It's funny. I almost didn't go either. One of my colleagues suggested I go. I really needed to get away, and I made an amazing decision. I met a wonderful man that treats me well and understands me. More importantly, you are patient with me and I really appreciate that so much. You have also helped me grow over the months in so many ways. I can't thank you enough for that. I have a different perspective on life."

"You are most welcome. My mom always said:

Change your thinking one thought at a time. Change your life one day at a time."

The two of them finished their dinner and walked back to the B&B. They stopped along the way to pick up a bottle of wine. They arrived back to their suite to find vanilla scented candles burning with the windows open to allow the cool breeze to flow throughout the entire suite.

"Here's to us, a wonderful time of sharing" Pearson proposed.

"Nice. You are always a man with the right words" she replied.

"I have a surprise for you."

He sat on the bed as she took a silk scarf and blindfolded him.

"You can't touch. You hands have to remain on your lap and definitely no peeking."

"Agreed."

She went into the other bedroom and changed into a seductive crimson negligee. She brought a basket of strawberries and dipped them in chocolate as she rubbed them over his lips but he couldn't bite. She dipped her finger in the chocolate and smeared it onto his lips for him to taste. She then smeared chocolate on his neck and chest and licked it off. Finally, she fed him a chocolate dipped strawberry and gave him a passionate kiss to taste the chocolate on his lips. Julie sucked his earlobes, licked his face, and sucked his fingers one by one. At that point, she removed the silk scarf so she could look into his eyes. His desire for her was at a peak as he rolled her over onto the bed, caressing her firm breasts working his way down to her treasure. He tasted her. She moaned. The two of them became one as their storm creates the quite eventually ending in an intimate slumber.

Julie woke to a mind filled with anxiety and regret. Her thoughts were haunting as she came to grips with the idea that she knowingly agreed to allow a stranger to watch her and the special man in her life to engage in their most intimate and private moments of sharing. She found herself questioning her judgment and morals. How could she have allowed this situation to get so far out of hand? Her parents taught her better she thought. What was the driving motivation for her not to do the right thing of accepting the responsibilities or consequences connected with her actions? She should have known better than to put herself in such a precarious position in the first place. Her weak moment of the flesh spun into a tangled web of deception. Julie promised Pearson she wouldn't keep secrets from him that could affect their relationship. After all, of this, could she really be honest with him going forward? How could she build a solid relationship when she continues to keep things from him?

After a few days had passed, she could no longer live with herself. She had to tell Pearson. She had fallen for him and honestly believed he had fallen for her. Her marriage was all but over and she didn't want to start a new relationship built on dishonesty and mistrust.

As she picked up the phone to call Pearson to meet in person, the phone from the package rang.

"Julie that was some kind of show you put on the other night. I wouldn't have pegged you as an actress. I'm impressed," the distorted voice cynically replied.

"What do you want from me," she replied in a voice filled with emotions.

"There is no need to be upset. Remember, I like to watch. Besides, if I really wanted to destroy you I could have done that already. I got what I wanted as I always do. You life will soon become less complicated."

"That's easy for you to say. You have no idea what I've been through recently. I can't take this anymore. I'm going to the authorities. I'm going to face my reality. Whatever happens, I will deal with it. I can't continue living like this," she said with tears in her eyes.

Julie, I told you. Things have a way of working themselves out," responded the distorted voice before hanging up.

Over the next few weeks, Julie didn't receive any more phone calls from the "blackmailer". As she prepared for her divorce hearing, her attorney called.

"Julie, are you sitting down?" he said in an overly excited voice.

"What is it now?"

"I heard from your ex-husband's attorney and they've agreed to all our terms. Apparently, your ex-husband is prepared to settle on the terms of the divorce and provide an additional $1000.00 in child support."

"Is this some sort of sick joke?"

"Not in the least." I have received the terms from the other attorney's office. It's confirmed," her attorney responded in an effort to calm his client down.

Julie was so relieved she didn't know what to say.

"Thank you," As she hung up the phone.

Later that week, she received an email and a phone call about an upcoming Board of Directors meeting. She prepared for the worst. She remembered what the "blackmailer" told about how the compromising pictures could possibly end up in the hands of the Board of Directors. The night before the meeting, she typed her letter of resignation and was prepared to present it to the Board.

When she reached to the conference room, the reception surprised her.

Winton Elliot, the Chairman, welcomed her into the room.

"Julie Barber, I want to congratulate you on a job well done. Apparently, you impressed a very influential donor during the Los Angeles Hospital Administrator's Conference back in the spring. The individual donated $10 million dollars on your behalf to the hospital for R&D under a couple of conditions. One, you will receive a ten percent compensation increase effective immediately. Secondly, the hospital will name the Eastern Wing Corridor on the 37th floor The Julie Barber Hall of Leadership 'A woman willing to take responsibility for her actions.' Julie, I don't know how you did it but on behalf of the Board of Directors, we sincerely thank you." Winton commended. Julie was speechless. This was the last thing she expected. She gracefully accepted the recognition from the Board of Directors.

* * *

Jonathan Westin called Pearson to meet for lunch. The two hadn't worked closely together in months. Pearson's contractual agreement to buy back Jonathan's company equity interest was fast approaching. Pearson worked hard to position himself financially to complete the deal.

"Pearson, how are things going?"

"They are going well. How is the buyout preparation coming along?"

"Things are good. I have financing all lined up with my Letter of Intent to complete the transaction.

"Excellent."

"Now that business is out of the way, how are things in your personal life?"

Honestly, things couldn't be better. I met this wonderful woman at the L.A. conference. I like her a lot. We connect on so many levels. She's been through a lot over the last few months personally but things have recently gotten better."

"Sounds good. What's that special lady's name?"

"Julie Barber. Do you know her?"

"Actually I met her at the conference. She seems nice. She is a special kind of woman from what I have seen and heard," Jonathan replied.

"Pearson it was good catching up. Give me a call closer to the time for the buyout."

"Thanks, I will."

Things did get better for Julie and Pearson. She finalized her divorce and moved on emotionally with her life. They continued to date and spend time together sharing hot passionate moments. Julie couldn't help but wonder if the person that took the pictures and made the calls had anything to do with how things turned out at work and in her divorce. The person did say things wouldn't be complicated for her.

Jonathan never told Pearson that he knew Julie in a less than appropriate way. Jon felt it was best that they both believed things had worked themselves out on their own. Knowing the truth was fine as he continued his search for the next entertaining venture. He savored the thoughts of watching the two of them. This would be the secret behind the truth.

THE ADVENTURE

March 7, 2010

I am Frank Lee Speaking and I deliver.
No signature required.

I want to take a few minutes to take your
mind on a journey. A journey based on words
that carry meanings that may weigh heavily
or lightly depending on where you are.

This journey entails an adventure and an exploration,
like Marco Polo, or Lewis & Clark but this adventure is
different for it's done in the light and not in the dark.

I met her along the way and that
in itself was the beginning.

Once again, I met her, but couldn't forget
her for she turned my head without

me looking.

For what I saw was a surprise, took me off balance
but I soon realized. This woman is different.

The story continues, as I didn't get far.
We met in the park but never in bar.

I said I'm Frank Lee Speaking and I
deliver. No signature required.

She said her name was Summer, but I thought
she was some-thing else. Her persona caught
my attention and she wasn't even fishing.

Her eyes were dazzling and charming, for they
had me trained like Pavlov's dog or Fe Fe, the
circus poodle. Speak, sit, roll over, and eventually
beg were the commands I played in my mind's
theater with three acts-no intermission.

I was stunned, done and on the run, like
a cheetah chasing wildebeest; but I wasn't
sure if I was the prey or the pursuer.

I quickly gained my composure and concluded that
I must seize the moment to connect with summer
but once again, I called her some-thing else.

I made moves on her like chess pieces
on a board: calculated, crafted

and concise.

Soon she was feeling my vibe and feeling
me—like I'm feeling for you, you, and
you! However, I can't reach you!

I am Frank Lee Speaking and I deliver.
No signature required.

Now Summer springs into action as she falls for
me. For it wasn't the physical for that is easily
achieved but Summer desired the emotional, sensual
but not necessarily sexual nourishment to fuel her
vessel or boat within her river of her passion.

Summer enjoyed our adventure for it was different.

My hands were constantly on her smooth brown
skin exploring the contours of her womanly
features—from her twin peaks forming a ridge, to

the flatlands—down her treasure trail to the edge of her tavern of passion. I embraced her treasure like a Caribbean buccaneer—tasting her like the sweet rum of the islands—in the figurative sense of course.

Because, I'm Frank Lee Speaking and I deliver. No signature required.

But wait, there is more. Summer liked me because my words tantalized and teased her imagination. I gave her what she wanted; I gave her what she needed. There was no discussion, contemplation, or uncertainty—no points required to be pleaded.

My words fed her inner desires like a culinary specialist—in and out, in and out of the oven or the range making sure the temperature was adequate and accurate in case I needed to make a change.

The more I delivered, the more she craved as a sensual refugee trapped in a desert environment.

I was her captain and I commanded her man in the boat like Columbus commanded the Piñata, Niña, and Santa Marina; but I didn't rediscover America for there were other rewards I cherished more.

I took Summer to new boundaries and new heights!

Quenched her sensual thirst and maximized her delights!

No stone was left unturned for I wanted to take her over the waterfall without her falling or getting hurt.

I could go on and on like Ponce de Leon searching for the fountain of youth,

Instead, she tasted the nectar that lit her desires
that created an eruption resulting in fires.

For Summer finally acknowledged
the things she desired,

Admitting to everyone that she loved the man that
speaks and delivers with no signature required.

Romantic Senses

November 7, 2010

Soft gentle kisses. Life is good when you mature
to a point when a kiss is the glue that sticks to
your inner soul. Memories that make a woman
feel young even when she has gotten old.

These words will make a girl weak in the
knees. I just say the simple words that make
you tingly, tantalizing with a bit of a tease.

Come with me on a verbal session, as I share my
expressions designed to reach your mind. My
words will be soft, subtle, and romantic as our
thoughts become intertwined. Feel the feeling, from
the floor to the ceiling as I whisper in your ear.

My words will have you yearning, as your
passion is burning with combustion without
the flames. Opposites attract meanings you will
extract, as I change the rules of the games.

Our eyes did meet, because no words did we speak,
but the story was already told. The way we connected
was flawless and impeccable, like a hand to a glove
as I looked through the windows of your soul.

Meeting for the first time is always a
significant event. I am captivated by all
facets: sights, sounds, and the scents.

Your lips I want to taste, my heartbeat's above

pace and all these are in my mind. I would behave differently but in life, there is only play, no pause or stop buttons and definitely no button for REWIND.

I'm out of my comfort zone—uncertain of the situation and emotionally displaced. I just smiled, remained calm and poised in order to save face. I moved through the transition, established a new position in order to make my move. You responded favorably, communicated effectively, as we established a collective groove.

Sometimes in life, we must live on the edge and occasionally take a chance. You turned my head, hypnotized by your vibe that all started with just one glance.

Your Poet

August 10, 2010

I am not your lover but your poet. I write to recite the words that may excite stimulate your mind while I give you a delight.

Feel my words touching your inner desires as they roll off my tongue like drops of dew in the morning. Do you hear my whispering voice like the autumn breeze as the seasons change?

From cool breezes to cool thoughts, they are needed to lessen the intense heat from your intimate passionate thoughts wondering uncontrollably throughout your mind and imagination.

Whether you are reminiscing of past lovers or creating scenes for an on-going fascination of hopeful thoughts to personify and come to fruition, it's the words, the thoughts, and the desires that create your reality.

Who am I? Who is the strange man that you haven't met or just met that appeal to your intimate ideas, teasing your most personal thoughts, and speaking to you as if he has always known you?

You may ask yourself. Why does he say the things that I may think, appeal to emotions that I don't show because they may expose my vulnerabilities or inhibitions? You may be torn between accepting the words that create the pictures that feed your innermost ideas that nurture your spirit and enrich you on so many levels.

On the other hand, you may be rejecting my words because they give you an uncomfortable feeling of vulnerability violating the self-preservation measures designed to protect your inner core of existence.

Whichever the case may be, I am your poet not your lover unless you desire me to be one in the same.

THE ROMANCE

April 20, 2012

Who says romance is dead? It lives deep within us as
I share with you. Holding hands, making plans as our
imagination grandstands the things we love and enjoy.

Hold you close. Pull you near. Whisper your name
and soothing words softly in your ear. There won't
be any touching just teasing. You will have to enjoy
this experience through your other senses outside of
the obvious one of touch. The walks, the talks and
any time spent fill my questions with your answers.

You should hold on to the moment and me. How so?
Tightly, loosely, and moderate are the responds. Hold
tightly so I don't slip through your fingers but loose
enough for me to catch my breath, as it gets shorter
when I'm near you. Holding moderately should be
your final answer because anything, as long as it's in
moderation, is fine to indulge in every once in a while.

Sometimes it's hard to put things into words, think,
or share emotions especially those emotions that
are succulent as your favorite but forbidden fruit.

So go ahead and taste the sweet thoughts of
my imagination as I share them with you.

WE GO RIDING

March 17, 2011

The top is down as the breeze blows through your
hair. It's a warm spring day and its sun everywhere.
Even with the top down, baby, I can still smell your
perfume. The aroma is mixing with warm spring air
creating a combination that draws me closer to you.
As you're looking off into the distance, I'm admiring
your side view as it creates a focal point in my
moving painting by the sea. The seashore is the
background as the surf meets the soft smooth sands.
Your sundress does so many things for your
curvaceous body as I appreciate each individual
curve and contour hypnotizing me in unison as
I drive down this winding road along the sea.
Oh, my! Baby you have way too much thigh for my
eye as I struggle to keep my eyes on the road.
I want to touch you but I can't. It's too strong for I
know your presence would consume my remaining
self-control. My focus struggles to maintain direction
as we ride on our way to no particular destination.
As I touch your leg to get your attention, you have
already captured mine by being in your presence.
Time goes quickly as we share our moments but
stands still when I'm away. It's the little things that
may go unmentioned or unnoticed but when I'm
with you, my focus struggles to maintain direction
as we ride on our way to no particular destination.

My Story

May 16, 2014

Sitting in another boring training class
or was it another boring seminar.

I'm not sure or I don't remember. Really, what I
meant was I was wrestling with apathy, ignorance,
and a passive perspective: I don't know, I
don't care, and I am not trying to find out.

What I do remember is when she walked into
the room. All the Ws popped in my head:
Whoa, wow and what in the world?

She didn't walk but strolled to the
rhythm of music that only I heard.

Tight fitted skirt, long legs, and a silk blouse
showed all her favorite curves and mine too.

Her mouth moved, my mind wondered.
What was wrong with this picture?

I wasn't sure if I was epileptic or reverting
back to my neo-natal days of one piece, bibs,
and breast-feeding. Drool rolled down my
chin until there were puddles on the floor.

I would have drunk her bath water
through a slurpy straw.

Nevertheless, let me digress. I'm Frank Lee Speaking.

I regained my poise and pulled my swagger out of

my pocket like a pistol in knife fight. She had crossed
the line not blurred the line by killing my coolness.

I took her to school, made her drive, and pay for
the gas. I taught her lessons she couldn't learn.

I cleared the books off the table and did her like my
homework breaking her down like improper fractions.

After I ripped off the lace mask covering her
treasure, I ran through her niceness like a sexual
villain. She was the beauty and I was the beast
but this wasn't a cartoon or a stage play.

I grabbed and pulled a big handful of hair. Every
time I tugged, she moaned, changing gears as
I gave her more throttle like my racecar.

She arched her back and breathed irregularly. I
wasn't sure if she would tap out or be knocked out.
I folded her up like fresh clothes out the dryer.

I panted and growled while she whimpered
like a new puppy in a new place.

I brought the thunder until it was summer
rain flooding her passion pond with the
juices of excitement and release.

[Clean up on aisle 3, make it aisle 4 as well.]

Then it hit, actually, my colleague
nudged me for I had dozed off.

All my thoughts were just that: thoughts. This
is just another example of a mere hypothetical
reference without the possibility of reality.

That is my story and I'm sticking to it.

I Learned

I will paint the sky your favorite color or I will call
you in the middle of the day for two reasons: to hear
your voice and to let you know how you dominate
my thoughts. I am all man. How long, how far, or how
deep are just a few questions to describe what you get!

Boardrooms or boardwalks: I'm comfortable on both.

Time spent with me for the rest of your
life will be the best of your life.

One action always overshadows 1000 spoken words.

Looks change lives.

Loving the right woman should be as easy
and relaxing as watching lily leaves lying
lazily on lakes. I see the morning sun dancing
between leaves peeking through the trees as I'm
peeking through the window of your heart.

I have two questions: Is there room for
me in there; will you invite me?

With a good woman, a man can do great things.

I chose my words, but you finish my sentences.

You chose your thoughts, but I read your mind.

I held your hand because I knew you were afraid.

I Learned

I took you out of your comfort zone
because you needed to grow.

You told me to hold on because you knew
I was emotionally falling down.

You listened when I wasn't talking.

I listened when your actions spoke.

Men, look for a good woman not a good time.

Women, look for a man that builds you
up when life and others tear

you down.

THE ESSENCE OF TOUCH

April 11, 2010

As I stroll down the aisle of my mind shopping
through my thoughts, I came to the realization
that all women are unique whether they
are full-figured down to the petites.

As the wind blow, so will my words flow to
and through your ear lobes down to your
mind's canvas painting a picture like De
Vinci, Van Gogh or Michelangelo?

I want you to feel the essence of my touch: Not by my
hands like any other man but through your desires and
imagination like the matrix or Alice in Wonderland.

I want you to cherish my touch when I'm not
there and remember the time we spent, the places
we went, and all the funny gestures and

outrageous comments.

See, the things I say may take you places you
don't go, express emotions you can't show,
and teach you things you didn't know.

I am to lead, not necessarily to follow; because I
always love a woman's mind, body, and spirit,
which will never leave her feeling hollow.

My words create laughter and laughter creates
the life that we have to live—For as a woman,

you can't be positioned to receive if I'm not poised, postured and in a positioned to give.

However, today my words won't sexual, but highly intellectual and on a different level that you have seen thus far. For the journey I'm taking you on will be limousine style riding not your regular everyday commuter car.

I want you to feel the words I'm saying, not the regular band rehearsal tunes of everyday reality people are often playing.

I know you thinking about all the things that I have been saying and realize that my words are concise, sincere, and genuine and not the regular words games people are often playing.

That is why I take my time as I lay out my rhymes to share my vibe and my flow. My words are intended to be soothing with a sense of quiver or something highly desired, but I will stop at this point, because I'm Frank Lee Speaking and I deliver and as always—no signature required.

MY VIBE

April 20, 2010

As I venture on my travels across this fertile land,
I am discovering lots of new experiences.

As the temperatures peaks, the birds tweet, people
often creep, as we become high temperature
misfit, better known as "desert freaks."

My mind tells me that being naughty is a better
feeling than feeling like good is my only option.

My style is simple as I deliver my flow to a special
lady. Are you that special lady? My words are
intended for your gray matter because that's all
that really matters. I intend to break into your
imagination, connect with your inner thoughts and
make passionate love to your inner sensuality.

I want to whisper my words in your ear until
it sound like your mind's voice urging you to
bring your sensual thoughts to fruition.

Do you feel my strong but gentle hands rubbing all over
your body in the love scene of your mind's movie?

If you do, then you will know my hands are going
up and down your back running my fingers
through your hair as I pull you close to kiss your
sensual lips above and below your navel.

Feel me breathing on your neck as my arms

embrace you with a warm hug that shows you
that I want to take it to the next level. I know this
is an evolution and escalation of the situation.

Our words and our thoughts will continue our mingling
until your juices build, flow with of bit tingling, for I
haven't physically touched you; it's all a mental thing.
Hear my soft words that touch your mind's palette and
tease it like a small spoonful of your favorite dessert.

I'm swimming through your delectable stream of
fascination but never getting tired following the
current until we both go over the waterfall.

However, as I mentioned before in the essence of touch,
I will take you places, have you making different faces,
as well as leaving sensual traces of me on your mind's
playground. The emotions you show only I should
know as your teacher keeping you after school.

The emotions you show only I should know
as your teacher keeping you after school.

You will enjoy my sessions as I give you lessons
to teach you things may or may not already know.
However, if you are naughty and misbehaving,
you, I will be spanking, me, you will be
thanking for my mental vibe and my flow.

A WOMAN

November 2, 2010

We have been talking for so long.

I could make you laugh; you can cry on my shoulders
and just be a woman with no inhibitions.

If you think that is sweet, I'm serious, as I
know how important it is for a woman to be
held. Part of being a true woman is having her
"me" time. As a poet, I recognize your inner
thoughts as we connect on so many levels.

Do you hear my voice with a southern
accent that gives you southern comfort
like a vacation bed and breakfast?

I am the journey and the vacation because of the
soothing feeling I will give you. I can be with you
in so many ways and tell you "you got me".

The inner connection is the most intimate. The
touch, the look, and the sense of comfort are the
powerful collections for the essence of warmth.

Every woman is special is so many ways. As she goes
through things in life, the man's bond for her should
be built so she can weather any emotional storm.

Come to me; run to my strong but comforting
arms so I can shelter you from that "big bad
world" even if it's just for a moment. That moment

may be what you need. My words will give you that reassuring edge to survive another day.

All women are bold and powerful but you won't need your cape with me. With me, you can be you as you embrace your "me" time. Because sometimes, a woman just wants to be a woman.

THE STORM

March 15, 2014

Lightning flashes! Thunder rumbles!
Moreover, the summer rains. After we
are soaked, does it really matter?

Gentle, tropical winds are sometimes warm,
wet, and steamy but without the sand.

I know what makes your prize a treasure. I can taste it
like a ripe peach in my mind. The sweet juices exceed
my mental expectations captivated by the raw intensity
of thunder and rain. Our storm creates the quite.

This is a sign of maturity painted by
consciousness—a kiss, a look,

a touch.

It is the touch without the hands. Giving is an
obvious choice, not an incentive. It is a simple
desire—holds your hand; warm your heart; run my
fingers through your hair as I look into your eyes.

My eyes met yours without the
need for an introduction.

Feel you next to me!

Smell your scent!

Hear your laughter!

Embrace your presence!

The Storm

After every storm, summer rain is the glistening
mist suspended against a gray background.
The hues of crimson, amber, and emerald
act as an explanation point reminding me of
a new beginning. A rainbow is tied to

a gift.

Water blue, sky blue—there is no
clear line of separation.

What Makes It Hot?

May 1, 2012

Do you have to ask? Oh, this ride is going to be hot and steamy. There is going to be a lot a teasing, pleasing resulting in a lot of stress relieving. I can smell you and I don't mean your perfume. I'm taking over, as a man should do. This is my message to you. Are you feeling me like I feeling, smelling and eventually tasting you?

Oh, we are going to make a movie that the kids can't watch and mommy and daddy wouldn't approve.

I'm sweating, you're moaning from the heavy petting and I'm running my strong hands through your hair. You want me to dominate you don't you? You want a man that is bold and strong with the skills to take you deeper, make you hotter, wetter as I stroke your ego among other things. Come with me. We can do it your way. I'm taking you to the edge until you surrender your remaining self-control releasing your inhibitions. Our tongues touch, teasing your hot wet mouth, down the back of your neck. I see you shivering but you won't be cold.

Again, I ask, what makes it hot? Your fingers in my mouth, sucking them one by one as I look into your eyes before I turn you around so you can feel me breathing on the back of your neck as I run my hands along the inside of your thighs. I can feel your tension building. Do you want me to touch it? I will touch you only if it's hot and wet.

Again, what makes it hot?

LIVE YOUR LIFE FOR YOU, ALL OTHERS ARE SPECTATORS

"THIS IS NOT what I wanted to be when I grow up," as he wiped the sweat from his forehead. "All these boxes, I'm already behind on my deliveries. I have so much work to do today and I'm running out of time." Anthony Harrison's life had changed a lot over the last 8 years. He had gone from being a top engineering student to driving a logistics truck for a company that specializes in antiques and unique historical artifacts delivery.

Anthony Harrison was born to a hard working middle class family. His grandfather, Gustavo Harrison, an immigrant from Bermuda, came to the United States to get a good education and to pursue better work opportunities. His son (Anthony's father, Francisco) worked hard to earn a scholarship and eventually became a manufacturing engineer. Anthony's mother, Susan, was from the United States. Anthony's parents met in college and eventually married. Susan went on to become a librarian for the Truman Memorial Library in Manhattan, New York. The Harrison family valued getting one's education. Anthony's grandmother worked hard to earn her master's degree in Educational Leadership. She is a retired high school principal and music teacher. She still teaches part-time in Manhattan. Anthony and his brother, Simon, spent the summers with their grandmother when they were little boys. She always enjoyed their company as she taught them music and life lessons. Simon was more interested in science and math while Anthony expressed a keen interest in music. Their grandmother noticed Anthony's strong clear, sonorous voice. Anthony was a natural singer like his uncle.

Francisco never wanted Anthony to pursue singing. Anthony and his father had several contentious conversations about singing throughout Anthony's life. Francisco's oldest brother, Marshall, made poor decisions resulting in unfavorable paths throughout his life. Marshall loved and lived the "fast life." He enjoyed early success in the music industry. However, through negative influences, his life took a turn for the worst. Marshall's drinking habit went from having an occasional cocktail after shows to becoming so dependent upon alcohol that he couldn't perform on stage. From alcohol to drugs, Marshall's life soon spiraled out of control. From bad investments to poor relationship choices, Marshall's life fell apart almost as quickly as he had risen to stardom.

Francisco feared his son would suffer a similar fate or worst if he pursued a career in the music industry. He saw the whole industry as a pit of undesirables waiting to claim its next victim. He was extremely hesitant about the idea of Anthony becoming a professional singer. He selfishly wants his son to "follow in his footsteps" and become an engineer. His narrow-minded perspective and stubbornness prevented him from seeing any other point of view.

Anthony continued to excel in science and math in school but his heart was always into music. He was an excellent student; worked extremely hard; and earned a scholarship from Nova Institute of Technology. N.I.T. was one of the most prominent technical universities in the country. Things were going well for Anthony is school. He worked hard, enjoyed his classes, and made several friends. One of his friends, Chad, mentioned to him about an upcoming concert on campus and asked Anthony if he was going. Anthony never missed an opportunity to hang out with friends especially when it came to music.

"Tony, are you going to the concert?"

"What concert Chad?"

"Souls of Midnight," Chad replied.

"I've never heard of them. What kind of music do they play? You know I don't get out much for social events on campus."

"I know all so well. Tony, you have to get out more. I know studying and doing well in school are important. I get that, but you have to live a little."

"Man, you don't understand. My parents don't play that at all. I have to hear the story repeatedly about how my grandfather came to this country without any-thing but a few clothes and a driving desire for a better life. He left Flatter Village in Bermuda on a merchant vessel bound for Miami, FL with a final destination of Baltimore, MD. He was a cook on the ship in exchange for his room and board. He worked hard, moved around, and eventually settled in New York. That is where he met my grandmother. She was a schoolteacher at the time. They fell in love, had a bunch of kids (my dad being one of them), and grandkids, namely me."

"Wow, that's some story Tony, and it's amazing. I only asked if you were going to the concert." Chad replied as the two of them looked at each other and busted into laughter.

"I'm just letting you know what I have to deal with. It's not bad. I'm very proud. Education is a big thing in my family. I just don't want to let them down."

"I understand. Besides, there's going to be lots of girls at the concert. You know they like those singer types," Chad replied as he smiled and winked at Anthony.

"Wait, I'm one of those singer types. I got talent."

"Sure Tony, we all do."

"The band usually calls up a person from the audience to sing a few bars of a song to see who really has talent. It's a way to give those aspiring singers an opportunity."

"Man I would love that chance."

Anthony eyes got wide and his ears perked up when he heard that. It was an opportunity to sing and he loved to sing. It was in his blood. He thought he could display his talents with this opportunity maybe leading to something long-term. Worst-case scenario, the concert would feed his driving passion to sing.

Sure enough, Tony and Chad did attend the concert along with a few other friends. They all had a good time. The band was great. They arrived early so they could be close to the stage. Tony thought he needed to be near the stage in case he got a chance to sing.

The lead singer of Souls of Midnight announced:

"Who out there thinks they have talent. Who thinks they have what it takes?"

Tony raised his hand vigorously as his friends cheered him on. The lead singer picked him.

"Come on up here. What is your name son?"

"Anthony, Anthony Harrison but everyone calls me Tony.

"Tony, show me what you got," replied the lead singer.

Tony took the microphone, opened his mouth and out came a powerful but smooth voice. The drummer quietly played a slow soulful groove as the bass player joined.

Tony rocked the microphone for about thirty seconds as the crowd cheered. Chad was in awe. Anthony was so excited, as he left the stage.

"Tony, you've been holding out on me. I didn't know you had pipes."

"I tried to tell you," as he smirked with a smug face. A few girls winked and waved and Anthony waved back.

Anthony found other singing opportunities here and there while he was in college. He maintained his grades with music being his outlet. While visiting over the holidays, he had a long talk with his mother.

"Mom, what's going on with Dad?"

"I didn't want to tell you but your father has diabetes

and an enlarged heart. The doctors told him he could no longer work giving his condition. He didn't want to tell you because he knows how important school is to you. We don't have the money to continue paying for college and meet living expenses. When your father stops working, my salary won't be enough to cover the expenses."

Anthony knew what needed to be done. His father had made so many sacrifices for the family. It was time for Anthony to step up and be a man for his parents. He finished that semester and didn't return to school in the fall. He got a job to help with his family's financial burden. Although his father wanted him to be an engineer, his passion was to sing. It wasn't an ideal outcome but he really didn't want to become an engineer anyway. That was his father's vision for him.

***

Months turned into years as he continued to work to support his parents and younger brother. Simon wanted to go to college but feared he wouldn't have an opportunity given the financial situation. He earned some scholarships, planned to work and borrow the rest. Simon worked hard as well to make things happen and helped his parents so they wouldn't lose their house.

By this time, Anthony was working two jobs to make ends meet. He worked at an IT helpdesk and drove a delivery truck. The global logistics company he worked for specialized in the delivery of antiquities and specialty items. Based on the delicacy of the item, the company required recipients to sign for all deliveries.

Anthony had a package delivery out in the suburbs to a: Carissa Theopolis.

***

Carissa Theopolis is the oldest of three children. Her younger brother and sister are fraternal twins. With a heritage of Greek and Portuguese, she has brown eyes, long brown hair, bronze colored skin that accents her Mediterranean features. Carissa also has curvy hips and long legs courtesy of her mother's Portuguese descent. She is active and maintains her fitness through yoga, palate, and running. Carissa grew up in an upper income family. Her father is an investment banker and runs the family owned investment firm that specializes in business acquisitions in the medical industry. Her mother is an intellectual property attorney for a global media firm with a regional headquarters in New York.

Exposed to the finer things in life, Carissa is a cultured and well-traveled woman. Having traveled all over Europe and the Mediterranean during summer vacations, she has a broad perspective on life. During her travels, she met many people and exchanged ideas through various conversations. Although an introvert, she is very open-minded when it comes to learning and talking to people about art and antiques even if she doesn't do most of the talking. She loves to experience the local people, visit museums, and historical sites.

With a bachelor's degree in fine arts, Carissa has eclectic taste in art, music, and antiques. An avid collector, her travels have afforded her numerous opportunities to purchase rare items. Often times, she would purchase these items in foreign countries and have a global logistics company handle the necessary arrangements to have the items delivered to her house.

Carissa's grandfather started the investment firm back in the 1960s with $500.00 dollars. Her grandfather is a warm, humble gentle spirited man. No one would ever know he is a multi-millionaire. He shows compassion, respect, and friendliness toward people as he connects with them on a personal level. Those were his core values when he started the firm, and he still believes these values today. "Rissa" as he often calls her is his oldest grandchild and possibly his favorite, but he would never tell anyone. She spent time with him when she was growing up. He never had a daughter so she was the daughter he always wanted. She loves her "Papa" as well. Unlike her parents, her grandfather was always supportive of the things she was interested in as long as those things were morally right. He often told her "live your life for you, all others are just spectators."

However, Carissa's parents are part of the elite social-economic class that often exist when there is a divide between the haves and the under privileged. Through the course of their business dealings and exclusive social circles, her parents had limited perspectives of others from different social economic backgrounds. Her father often subconsciously marginalized others not within his same income bracket. Her mother's competitive often-adversarial work environment left little room to 'play nicely with others.' Overall, her parents were borderline "snobs."

However, because Carissa traveled and had a broader perspective of people, coupled with her adopted grandfather's values, she didn't share her parent's philosophy regarding class differentiation. She felt that people were people regardless of their social status or income unless they proved otherwise. Specifically in her line of work, she dealt with individuals from various backgrounds and income levels. Carissa enjoys being an art broker. She handles all the various logistics connected with bringing the right people together to make things happen.

***

"Ma'am, SG Logistics, I have a delivery for you." Anthony said as he knocked on the door.

"I will be right there."

Carissa answered the door. Both of them were surprised. She didn't expect to see such a handsome deliveryman, and Anthony didn't expect to see such a beautiful woman.

"Can I get you to sign right here?"

"Sure. No problem."

"Thank you."

Carissa was truly surprised. She didn't know what to think. Maybe he is my regular delivery person in this area. She wondered if she would ever see him again; so many questions filled her head.

A few weeks passed and Carissa was expecting another package, a vase. Anthony delivered the package, knocked on the door, and announced himself, in accordance with company policy.

"Hello Ms. Theopolis."

"Call me Carissa. You've been delivering packages to me for weeks now."

"Yes ma'am, Ms Carissa Theopolis."

Carissa laughed.

"How long have you been driving delivery trucks?"

"Are you referring to today or in general," as he paused and then smiled.

She smiled back.

"I see you are quick on your feet Anthony."

"How do you know my name?" He replied.

"It's on your name tag." She pointed.

They both laughed and had a brief conversation before Anthony was off to his next delivery.

A few weeks later, Carissa received several packages this time.

"You are really popular today."

"I know—no autographs only photographs today!" she smirked as they both laughed.

"I see you are funny. That's a good thing in a woman. Where is Mr. Theopolis?"

My father is home with my mother—well he's probably at work now. If you are asking if I'm married, I am not. I am seeing someone."

"I'm not surprised; a beautiful woman that is charming, funny and witty. I didn't think you were available," Anthony replied as he grinned.

"Where is your wife?"

"I have no idea. I haven't met her yet."

"I'm still shopping," he grinned.

"I have to go. It's a busy day. I will see you next time."

"Ok, take care until next time."

Carissa was seeing someone, Winton Covington. Winton was the great grandson of William Covington Sr. William started his family's investment banking firm during the post Depression Era. He worked hard and kept the firm private throughout the years. Winton grew up in a privileged environment. He attended the finest boarding schools, private schools, and universities. Although well traveled, he expressed little interest in art. He leads his family's investment firm as its CEO. Winton loves the competitive nature of investment banking. Power, prestige and influence motivate him and dominate his life. Carissa met Winton at an art charity event. At the time, he appeared charming and interesting. However, since they have been dating, he seems to spend less time with her attributing this fact to his additional work demands. Her father likes Winton because they are both investment bankers. He mentioned one day that Winton would be a good addition to the family. Carissa believes this desire is about business. She can't prove it. It's just a feeling she has.

***

Carissa ordered an item on purpose so she could see Anthony again. The package arrived.

"Hi Anthony, how are you today?"

"I'm well. I'm just busy as usual."

"You mentioned you were in college. What were you studying? Did you graduate?"

"I was studying engineering at N.I.T. but I had to drop out to take care of my family."

"Do you have children?"

"No. My father became ill and was unable to work. The loss of income was devastating to my family and we couldn't afford to keep me in school. Besides, my little brother wants go to college so I made the sacrifice so he can attend. I really didn't want to be an engineer. That was my father's vision for me."

"Wow. That is a lot of responsibility. What do you want to be?"

"I want to be a singer. I am going to be a singer. My dad doesn't support my dream because my uncle was a singer and lost his way. My father doesn't want me to suffer the same fate."

"I understand. My Papa always said—live your life for you, all others are just spectators."

"I like that. That makes a lot of sense."

"Do you sing anywhere now?" she inquired.

"Yes, I sing at a little 'hole in the wall' place every Thursday. I'm preparing for this upcoming singing contest. If I win, I get $200K and a record deal. You should come hear me perform sometime."

"I would like to but it's complicated. I have social pressures I have to uphold." She replied with hesitation.

"I get it. I know you can't be seen in a blue-collar establishment. That would significantly hurt your public image." He replied cynically.

She frowned.

"I didn't mean it like that."

"I'm sorry. That was insulting. If you change your mind, here is the address and my number."

She thought long and hard. She questioned her values and perspective. Maybe she had become an elitist. Carissa didn't think she shared her parent's philosophy when it came to her views of people. Perhaps she was a product of her environment at this point.

She called her friend Jennifer.

"Hey Jen, what are you up to?"

"Not much. What's new with you? How are you and Winton doing?"

"We are ok. I met this guy. He seems nice. He sings at this place in Queens on Thursdays.

"Guy? Queens! What's really going on?"

"He is the delivery guy for the company that ships a lot of my antiques. He sang for me briefly but I really want to see him sing but you know how my family is."

"Well, I do understand and if you really want to go, I have a plan."

"Really—what is it?"

"You wear dark glasses and borrow one of my wigs and no one will probably recognize you."

Carissa laughed at the plan but then she reconsidered the idea that this plan might just work. The next Thursday, the two of them carried out Jennifer's plan. They arrived at *Jake's*. The place was tucked away off a main street. Parking was extremely tight. The valet asked Carissa and Jennifer if they knew where they were going. Each of them looked puzzled as they said simultaneously, *Jake's*. Once inside, they both were surprised at how nice the decor was. There was Jazz art on the wall, pictures of various celebrities that had visited, old sheet music from the Big Band Era, vinyl records on the wall, and a picture of Jake. The place had a quaint cozy feeling for relaxing and enjoying good food, drinks and music.

They sat in the back. Carissa felt so uncomfortable fearing someone would recognize her. Anthony soon hit the stage and warmed up with the other musicians. Anthony is a fantastic singer she thought as she listened to him sing song after song. She didn't realize how talented he was until she saw him perform in person. The show was amazing as Anthony left the crowd cheering for more. His presence on stage captivated her. Because Carissa didn't want to take the chance of accidently running into him, she and her friend left early.

She called Anthony the next day to let him know she had seen him perform.

"Hi Anthony, how are you?"

"May I ask whose calling?"

"It's Carissa Theopolis."

"Oh hey, I'm surprised you called. How are things going?"

"Things are going well. I changed my mind and I saw you perform last night. I'm impressed. You are a very good singer. Jennifer and I decided to check you out.

"I do my best"—he grinned.

"I want to see you but not while I'm at work. How about us meeting for lunch this Saturday?"

She accepted, and he called her later with the details.

The two of them were walking through the park late one afternoon when a passing rain shower caught them by surprise. They ran seeking shelter from the immediate downpour. They were soaked as they laughed over the exhilarating event until their eyes met and lips connected. This was their first passionate kiss as the summer shower soaked their skin but raised their passion and chemistry. The rain served as a catalyst—escalating the obvious chemistry between the two. Anthony held her close in his arms as their bodies became one. He quenched her emotional thirst and escalated his desire for her to a completely new level. She could feel his temperature rising in spite of the cooling sensation of the summer rain. Anthony gave her things a man couldn't buy for her and things she couldn't buy on her own: caring, warmth, and a sense of appreciation.

They met for lunch at a quiet eatery in Queens. Because Anthony was a driver, he knew several places the two of them could be away from the mainstream popularity of Who's Who. Carissa could maintain her discretion and he could spend quality time with her without the worries of exposure.

Weeks turned in months as the two grew closer. He took her to dinner one night to a cozy Italian restaurant. It was a small quaint eatery, even smaller than her living room. The aroma of pasta, olive oil, and garlic filled the air teasing her nose and appetite as soon as she walked inside. The food was delectable as she savored each bite. From the garlic bread, to the Rigatoni with cheese and Italian sausage, her entrée, and the other dishes she sampled were unbelievable. She was amazed how good the food was. She had traveled and enjoyed some of the finest restaurants in Rome, Venice, and Florence Italy but this food made her question if she was in Italy now. Anthony was entertained, as she tasted the appetizing cuisine. She was like a little child, unsure what she wanted to sample next. Carissa was almost full from just the samples. He told her that she could take a "To-Go" bag with her; it was normal for Luigi's.

They went for a walk after dinner. "I'm going to need to do palates for the next 6 days after eating all that food Anthony."

"You look fine, very fine." Anthony replied as he licked his lips.

"You are such a flirt." as she slapped him on the arm.

"My eyes don't lie. My mouth may but never my eyes," as he grinned.

"Sure, tell me anything."

Anthony took Carissa home. They both enjoyed the romantic evening of food wine, and stimulating conversation.

"Thank you for another wonderful evening. Would you like to come in for some coffee or brandy?" She asked.

"Yes, I would like that."

Carissa home was the prodigy of exquisite style and affluent taste. From the 8' mahogany doors throughout the house to various details of all furnishing, her house was a pristine example of style and luxury. Various paintings perfectly placed created multiple focal points to lead the viewer's eyes. The living room had a marble entrance in the foyer followed by a tightly knitted Persian rug accenting the earth tones of brown, olive, and bronze throughout the house. The color tones flowed from room to room; each room with an established personality. From rustic hardwood floors to Italian tile, each room was a unique experience as Anthony walked from room to room during his tour.

The kitchen exuded luxury but functionality. Dark speckled granite countertops were accent points for the pecan colored smooth cabinets with antique handles. The upper cabinets with stained frosted glass allowed some transparency but mainly served as a cue to indicate what rested behind the doors. A stainless steel refrigerator and oven established themselves as pillars in this executive chef style kitchen.

The rest of the house presented a warm relaxing atmosphere from custom drapery to a grandfather clock in the corner. Carissa's home accented her profession and appreciation of the arts.

The den with the fireplace was an excellent retreat and provided the ambiance for a relaxing conversation. The two sat down, poured a glass of brandy and continued the tête-à-tête from earlier in the evening.

"I always enjoy spending time with you. You are a special woman in so many ways. You bring out things in me I haven't experienced in years."

"Thank you. I always enjoy your company. I learn something new about you and in general every time we are together. I realize there are a lot of things I don't know but I'm open-minded."

Anthony held her close in his arms as they watched the red, yellow and orange colors of the ambers dance and crackle as the logs return to the ashes of the beginning. Shared romantic gazes, wine toasts and a warm fireplace were all gifts in the celebration of the arrival of the weekend.

Anthony put his glass down and held her face in his hands as he gave her a gentle kiss. Her lips were soft, sweet, and succulent like his favorite fruit. One kiss turned into another with the next one extending longer as they both savored the moment. He breathed on her neck as her perfume tantalized and invited him closer. His cologne was masculine complimenting his natural scent. He ran his fingers gently through her hair as he looked deeply into her eyes. Her eyes sent an invitation to come closer and touch her as a man is supposed to do: gentle but strong. Her presence had all but seized and consumed his remaining self-control. He nibbled on her ear as he whispered sweet nothings—"I want to taste you." She had goose bumps as he breathed on her neck. His strong hand rubbed the inside of her thigh as he kissed her passionately. Her breathing shortened as her intensity and anticipation increased. He licked her lips as she leaned back onto the oversized sofa while he pressed his strong manly body on top of her. Passionate kissing continued with heat and intensity as their bodies begin to move. She could feel his stiffness pressing against her sheer dress. His hands drove down the road of her womanly curves and contours; she enjoyed the ride. She gestured for him to let her up as she took his hand and led him down the hallway.

At the end of the hallway was her bedroom; an oversized canopy king bed with Egyptian linen, a Hungarian goose down duvet and duck down pillows. The two of them melted into the softness of the comforter. Their hot passionate kisses continued from the sofa. Anthony caressed and squeezed her soft nipples in his hands; sucking on the tips, swirling his tongue round and round. He sucked her nipples between his teeth and bit them gently as she moaned. He swirling his hot wet tongue on her nipples one by one, as she grabbed his head as her breathing shortened the faster he licked. He brought her to the edge of the bed as he rested on his knees. Her long slender legs rested over his shoulder as he discover places she didn't know existed. Anthony licked the back of her knees; along inside of her thighs; and the edge of her furnace. He asked her— "Do you want me to stop?"

"No," she uttered in a weak whispering voice.

Carissa was on fire. Anthony had already teased her with the appetizer. Now, she wanted the main course. However, he moved toward her dessert before his meal. Perhaps he didn't want to wait. He didn't. Anthony's tongue found its way to her special spot. Her pink love cave was neatly trimmed-throbbing in anticipation of his lip's first kiss. One gentle kiss led to another as he watched her every reaction. She flinched with each upward lick. His tongue traced the edges of her hotness.

His tongue teased her wet spot with each upward lick—gently gliding over her lips. She arched her back and opened her legs wider so there would be no obstruction. His fingers gently opened her soaked wet lips to taste her hot juices as he sucked on her throbbing clit. His tongue circled her pink hot button as he stuck his finger inside. Anthony's mouth covered her mound as his finger and tongue explored in unison in search of her G-spot. She grabbed his head, arched her back, and clenched her legs uncontrollably the deeper his tongue went inside while his finger rubbed over her G-spot. Her erotic cream began to flow as she lost control in anticipation. Her whole body pulsated and gyrated with each soft lick of his tongue until her juices exploded opening up the floodgates of desire. Carissa passed out for a few seconds from the intensity of her eruption. He cuddled her until she recovered and regained consciousness. His strong body rolled on top of her as he kissed to build her back to the edge of ecstasy. He entered her. She moaned as her body received him with ease. She was very wet as his hardness went deep inside. Slow, round and round motions followed in and out movements. He teased her by taking his pleasure rod. Her body pleaded for him to give it back to her. As he rubbed the tip of his manhood on her hot button of release, soft faint moans followed. Carissa aggressively rolled him over to get on top. She wanted to tame the wild stallion in her bed or at least enjoy the ride. Her fingernails dug into his chest as she rode uncontrollably, rocking back and forth. She reached another orgasmic milestone on the road to pure blissfulness. Only pausing for a few minutes as their bodies were soaked in sweat, Anthony turned her over to get on her back. He wanted her to feel his power. She arched her back to ease entry until their bodies connected in perfect rhythm. Slow and gentle moves set the stage to build the suspense of their epic movie. Anthony wasted no time going deep inside as she moaned. She arched her hips to surrender her body as she leaned her head back. He grabbed a handful of hair as the thrusts became more forceful. Soon, he was pumping her as he grabbed her shoulder with his other hand. She moaned with excitement and intensity with every thrusting pump.

"Faster!"

"Faster!"

"Faster!"

"Deeper!"

"Pull my hair!"

"Deeper!"

"Harder!"

"Harder!"

"Spank me!"

"Deeper!"

"Don't stop!"

"Don't stop!"

"Don't stop!"

[There was a brief pause.]

"I'm cuming baby," She yelled as her eyes rolled in the back of her head.

"I'm cuming too," As he growled and grunted.

They both went over the climatic waterfall without anyone getting hurt. Both struggled to catch their breath as the relief of release overtook their bodies. Their storm had created the quiet as the two drifted into slumber.

A few days later, Carissa called Anthony the day he was scheduled to deliver her package and pick up a custom chess set and table. The set dated back to 1722. A high-ranking Parliament member owned the set until his death. Generation after generation passed the artifact down. The family experienced financial hardship and had to sell the item. None of the family knew the real value so Carissa purchased the item at an international bazaar for an unbelievable bargain.

"Anthony, when you drop off my package, I have a package for a pick up as well. Can you take the item to your distribution center to be shipped?"

"Yes, I will be in your area around noon or so." He replied.

"I look forward to seeing you as always." she responded as her imagination ran wild.

As she relaxed on the sofa, she was still reliving each moment in her head and body. She imagined what it would be like for him to take her; dominate her at her house. She wanted raw intense sex. Her thoughts were unharnessed as she imagined him pulling her hair, bending her over her kitchen table. She wanted him and she wanted him now. He fed her inner desires as no other man had ever done. She could feel his presence; taste him, allowing her primal tendencies to take over.

Carissa answered the door wearing sandals, a skirt and a loose blouse.

"Hi Anthony! How is your day going so far?"

"It's going well but not too busy for a change. It's getting close to the slow season. I can use the break-no complaints from me."

"Have you had lunch yet? I made you a sandwich and packed you some fruit in a 'to-go" bag in case you don't have time." She replied.

No, actually, I haven't had lunch yet so this will come in handy," As he grinned and peaked into the bag. "Thank you so much."

"You are welcome. Did you want dessert?" As she rested her index finger on her lips as she gazed at Anthony in his uniform.

"Always!" as he fished around the bottom of the bag looking for the dessert.

"It's over here," as her fingers raised her skirt to show him her red lace panties.

"Damn! You are so bad all of a sudden. You do know I'm at work right.

"Yes, I do. How long is your lunch break?" as she walked toward him.

"I only get 30 minutes," Anthony replied.

"It won't take that long," as she pulled him to her kissing him passionately—positioning his hands on her soft round butt.

He grabbed her ass and squeezed it with one hand while grabbing a handful of hair with the other as she leaned against her kitchen table. She turned around and leaned over the table as he spread her long luscious legs. He unbuttoned his uniform pants, slide her panties to the side, and slide inside her wetness. She moaned and arched her back as he went deep inside. He pulled her hair with each forceful pump deep inside her sugar walls.

He went inside her fast, deep, and hard until she was slippery wet. She moaned louder the deeper he went. Both breathing heavily as their chests went in and out until their bodies were tense.

"Give it to me. Give me all of it. Pull my hair," Carissa huskily uttered.

"Yes! Yes! Yes!"

Anthony grunted and exploded as he released his hot load inside of her as she gasped for air. She moaned, jerked, and arched her back as she reached her climatic peak seconds after him. They both slumped over the table-covered in sweat radiating from a satisfying release knocking over a vase on the table.

What she thought was the vase hitting the floor was actually Anthony knocking on her front door. Apparently, she had drifted off waiting for him to arrive and dreamed the intimate episode.

"Are you ok? I've been knocking for a few seconds. I wasn't sure if you were sleeping."

"I drifted off for a moment."

"I hope you were dreaming of me," as he picked up the outgoing package.

"Maybe! Call me later."

"I will."

Carissa was still relishing in her intense and passionate episode with Anthony. This was an intriguing rendezvous even if it was all in her mind. She couldn't stop smiling as the scene played out vividly in her imagination.

***

On one of their strolls in Central Park, Winton's friend, Charles was walking his dog when he spotted Carissa and Anthony sharing an ice cream cone. As the two playfully licked the cone, Charles remembered Winton introducing him to her at a charity gala. He walked near them to get a closer look. It was definitely Carissa. Winton had mentioned to him that if things continue to go well, he would ask her to marry him. Winton saw the union between the two investment firms more as good business than marrying her for love. Once home, Charles called Winton immediately to let him know what he had seen.

"Winton, I'm just the messenger," Charles said, "So don't shoot the messenger."

"Are you and Carissa still together?"

"Yes, why you ask?"

"I just saw her in Central Park with another guy sharing an ice cream cone. They look pretty cozy."

"Thanks for telling me. I will talk to you soon."

Winton had been so busy over the last few months with an acquisition that his relationship with Carissa became the "sacrificial lamb." He was working 16 hours a day, 6 days a week with no slowdown in sight. He didn't notice she was emotionally thirsty. He assumed she understood the demands of his job and accepted this fact as part of their relationship. He often apologized and sent her flowers when he missed scheduled events.

Although she appreciated the flowers, she really wanted to spend time with him. Things became tense to a point where her frustration turned to resentment. She felt emotionally neglected. She cared for him but didn't want to appear selfish.

***

The chemistry between Anthony and Carissa was unfounded. They shared special and intimate moments. Things were going well but Carissa had concerns. She was already involved with Winton. However, he had left her emotionally thirsty over the last few months. She felt Anthony was really into her, which made the situation even more complicated. Something had to give.

The two of them got closer over the months. Anthony helped her form a new outlook on life. He showed her things from a working person's perspective; emphasizing the simple things in life, that money can't buy. Overall, Anthony was falling for her. Although she was from an affluent background, she was grounded, open minded, and receptive to different perspectives so he thought.

"Carissa, we been hanging out for some time now. How do you really feel about me? I know you were seeing someone when we first met. How serious are you two? Are you thinking of getting married? I don't want to continue seeing you if you're involved with someone else. I also don't want to be your little secret. I understand we are from different worlds and your family probably wouldn't think too highly of me. I may not be sophisticated enough for them—I want to know where I really stand."

She was silent. She didn't know what to say. She didn't expect this conversation today. She realized she couldn't toy with his emotions. She would be no better than her parents would: using people as if they were disposable commodities.

"You are right. I do have to sit down and make some hard decisions. I've really enjoyed the last couple of months. I always enjoy my time with you. You are funny, playful, outgoing and open minded. You don't judge—accepting me with all my flaws. You aren't like any other man I've ever dated. Will you give me a little time to sort things out?"

"Yes, I will give you some time but I won't wait forever."

"I know."

***

Winton was furious upon learning the information from Charles. How could she go behind his back and see another man? He rationalized that she should consider herself fortunate to be with a powerful successful businessman with the means to buy her anything she desires. He arranged a meeting to discuss and confront her.

"What is going on?"

"What do you mean," she replied.

"A friend told me he saw you in the park sharing an ice cream with another man. Is this information true? What's the meaning of this?"

"I was only having an ice cream. He is a friend. What do you care? You are only concerned about your acquisition. It's all about money with you. You don't spend any time with me anymore. I have asked you several times can we go out every once and a while. When was the last time we've been to dinner? I'm tired of being an entry on your calendar."

"I didn't realize you felt that way. I have been so consumed with this deal that I didn't think about how my work was affecting our relationship. I want things to work."

Carissa had a tough decision to make. Anthony is outgoing, playful and makes me laugh. Winton is caring, financially stable, and means well. Besides, my father likes him. Winton and I are also on the same economic level. We share similar backgrounds. If I chose Anthony, my family probably wouldn't accept him and that would cause conflict. She spoke to her mother to see what she thought.

"Mom, was Dad your first choice when it came to love?"

"Why would you ask that question?" She replied curiously.

"I was wondering. My best friend Jennifer is caught between two men."

"To be honest, there was a man before I met your

father. He was fun, exciting and outgoing. I didn't marry him even though we had a great time. I wanted the security and financial stability when it came to the future and a family. Money can't buy you love but love won't guarantee you a good future. I would advise her to choose the man with a stable future.

Carissa thought long and hard and decided she could no longer see Anthony. She called to arrange a meeting to tell him in person.

"Anthony thanks for meeting me. I know I asked for some time to let you know where we stood. I have made my decision. I can't see you anymore. This is best for both of us. We are from two different worlds."

"Do you love him?" He replied.

"Yes."

"Are you in love with him?"

"I'm not going to answer that question. I know you are hurt and I'm sorry."

"That's not fair. I deserved an explanation. Maybe this behavior is how wealth people do things. They just use people and then discard them when they are finished."

"Anthony, that is not true. I'm not like that at all."

"I can't tell. I hope things work out for you." He quickly turned and angrily walked away.

Anthony wasn't only hurt he was devastated. He wanted to get away from the situation. He felt like a fool—a pawn in an emotional game of chess.

A few weeks went by and Carissa order another

antiques for an upcoming sale. Expecting to see Anthony, she was surprisingly disappointed.

"Where is Anthony? I thought he delivered packages in this area."

"Ma'am, he requested a different area. He is still with the company. Is there a message I can give him?"

"No! Thank you for asking."

Heartbroken and hurt, Anthony refocused his attention and efforts. He had fallen for her. He admitted it to himself but he couldn't dwell on the situation. Anthony channeled his recent hurt and turned those volatile emotions into motivational fuel. The singing contest was six weeks away. Although he felt confident, he would be going up against fierce competition from Philadelphia to the Greater New York area. He really had to raise his game to the next level and beyond to be successful. The good news for him was that it was a relatively slow period at work. He was only working 40 hours a week instead of the normal 50-60 hours. This slow period allowed him additional time for rehearsal. It was normal for him to rehearse 6-7 hours per day after working an 8-hour shift.

After Winton's "wake up" call, things got better. He made time for Carissa. Although things weren't ideal, they were better. He genuinely made an effort once a week to do something with her. They usually went to dinner on Saturday Night to her restaurant of choice. In his mind, things were pretty much back to normal. The acquisition was weeks away from completion.

He promised her a big celebration when the deal was finally completed.

However, Carissa had a different point of view. She really missed the outings with Anthony. She missed that spontaneous interaction where she learned something new every time they were together. She was relaxed and open minded around him. She didn't feel her actions would be scrutinized which often happened with Winton. She didn't have to worry about conforming to the expected social norms based on her affluence and societal position. She wanted a normal life in that sense—the ability to make mistakes and grow from them without her life being under a "microscope."

More importantly, she missed the passion. Anthony took her places: emotionally, mentally, and sexually she had never been before and she loved it. He created a beast in the bedroom. She missed the emotional connection more than the physical part. However, she realized she had hurt him. She made her choice and now she had to live with it. As time passed, she rationalized to herself that she made the right decision.

Six months later, Winton asked her to marry him and she accepted. It was a gala affair. Carissa's father was excited to give his oldest daughter the wedding she always wanted. It was the social event of the summer. Hundreds of guests were invited. Her maid of honor and best friend Jennifer shared her special day. The weather was fantastic with numerous guests assembled outside in the Hamptons. Caramel colored roses throughout the wedding site created a storybook setting.

Carissa wore a white lace fitted dress with a four-foot train. The dress complimented her curvaceous figure. Her grandmother's pearls complimented her buxom twin peaks. She was beautiful on her special day. It was a joyous occasion with doves released; scented candles burned; and laughter filled reception halls.

***

The contest was only a week away. Anthony went to visit his grandmother. She had been his music teacher, inspiration, and biggest support of his music career.

"Hey Nana," he said in an upbeat tone.

"Hi Anthony, how are things coming along? I'm so glad to see you. You know I'm always glad to see you."

"How are you doing? What's new with you? How is teaching coming along with your students?"

"Anthony, what's going on? You know I know you too well and I know when something is on your mind. What is troubling you? You seem worried about something."

"Nana, you do know me so well. I have a lot going on these days. A woman I was interested in told me she didn't want to see me anymore. I thought she really liked me. We are from different backgrounds. She is from an upper income family and I believe she caved into the pressure of social expectations to be with a man she doesn't love. We had been seeing each other for a few months and I thought we connected. I guess I interpreted mixed signals—the wrong signals. In addition, on top of all of that, I have my singing contest coming up in a week. I believe I'm ready but it would really mean a lot if Dad would come to the contest and support me. I know he hasn't supported my dream to be a singer. He thinks I will end up just like Uncle Marshall. I only wish he would be my Dad and support something that I believe in with all my heart. He has never seen me sing in public. He has just been so obstinate. I only wanted him to be proud of me. I know I didn't become the engineer he always wanted me to be but I made a lot of sacrifices." He said as he dropped his head and turned away to look out the window.

"Do you love this woman?"

"Yes."

"Sometimes in life love is not enough. However, things happen for a reason and our paths in life are not straight lines. If things are meant to be, she will return to your life at the right moment and at the right time. I know you hurting. A broken heart leaves an empty feeling that only time can mend. As for the contest, you are going to do well. Remember the contest doesn't determine your success, you do. Winning may help but it's all up to you. Change your life one day at a time and lift your spirits with your own hands. You can 'build your wall of success one brick at a time.' You have your grandfather's island blood running through you, which means you have a lot of drive and determination. Your father loves you now and always has. He is protective of you and wants only the best for you. He is adamant about you pursuing singing because of what happened to Marshall. Marshall made his own decisions. It had nothing to do with singing. I don't think your father understands. I do believe one day he will come around, realize you are your own man, and respect your decisions. Sometimes, it takes time for parents to realize their children are adults, capable of making their own decisions."

"Thank you Nana. You always know what to say. I love you so much."

"I love you too. Regardless of what happens with the contest, I'm proud of you and so is your father."

Anthony hugged his grandmother and bid her farewell.

**

The day of the competition arrived. Anthony was prepared, poised, calm, and ready. The competition lasted all day. There were twenty-five contestants remaining based on the screening and elimination rounds. Soon it was down to three remaining finalists. The first two finalists sang with passion, fire, and intensity. The stakes were high and the competition was fierce at this point. Anthony was the last to sing. He replayed what Nana had said. 'This contest doesn't determine my success and I can build my own wall of success one brick at a time' were his thoughts before he walked out on stage.

Anthony opened his mouth and spoke. "Before I perform, this song is for my Nana. She taught me a lot and is still teaching me." Anthony sang as if singing was the air he needed to breathe. Every note was on point. His energy was explosive. The entire audience and building could feel his passion through his voice. He gave the audience a show they should have paid to see. The audience fed him energy and he reciprocated ten times over in return. When he finished, there wasn't a person in his/her seat. The standing ovation went on for at least a minute. He bowed and looked over to see his father standing off to the side. His father cheered, applauded, and gestured to him. Anthony was filled with emotions with tears in his eyes. Regardless of the contest outcome, he was overwhelm with joy that his father came to see him and finally supported his dream.

The judges awarded Anthony Harrison the grand prize of $200,000.00 dollars and a recording contract with Ventures, LTD. His life had truly changed and he had begun to build his wall of success one brick at a time.

"Dad, I didn't know you were coming. I'm so glad you came to see me. It's the best day ever." He said still filled with excitement.

"I had to come see my boy win this thang." He grinned. "Nana spoke to me and reminded me what was really important. I had to embrace the idea that this is your dream and passion and you have to follow it wherever it takes you. I know you will make the right decisions."

"Dad you raised us well. You made the sacrifices necessary for us to have the opportunities we have. I'm proud of you."

"I'm proud of you son. I always have been."

***

Anthony's singing career took off shortly. He went into the studio and recorded his first album in less than

4 months. He worked hard to make the most of this opportunity. The first few weeks of his album release yielded mixed results. This was a temporary setback. He was a little down but he kept working to market his album going from radio station to radio station to get the word out. After about six months, things began to turn. The album gained popularity on social media. Anthony's record label felt he needed to go on tour for a wider distribution outlet. He agreed.

The concert tour started in the U.S, which included 26 cities over the next 8 months. Anthony would be very busy but he didn't mind. It was his dream to share his gift with others.

***

Carissa had gotten used to married life. The deal finally closed and things in Winton's life got back to normal. He still worked a lot but not the crazy hours before the acquisition. After the company's purchase, he took Carissa to the French Rivera for two weeks. They also visited Monaco and chartered a yacht while in the area. They were living the life of luxury. A few weeks after their return, Winton suggested that the two of them celebrate a long weekend on the West Coast. It would be good to get away from the cloudy cool weather of NYC. She agreed. Winton arranged for a private jet to whisk them away. They would be cruising at 45,000 feet enjoying champagne and fruit. He booked the presidential suite at an exclusive boutique hotel in a private club. This would be the ideal get-a-away weekend. The day they were scheduled to leave, one of Carissa's clients called looking for an extremely rare item. Carissa had purchased a Ming vase months earlier when she was in Singapore. There were only five vases like this one in the world and she possessed the only one in North America. Anthony delivered that same vase a few months ago. She thought back to him. The vase was an ironic reminder when she and Anthony used to have brief conversations when her deliveries arrived. Her client wanted the vase shipped to her that day. She had already transferred the funds to Carissa's account.

"Winton, I have to make sure this vase goes out today. I know you have the plane booked but I have a commitment to my client. I hope you understand."

"Yes, I know and understand. I know that is part of your business. Do you want me to cancel the trip?"

"No, go ahead and I'll just catch a later flight and meet you at the hotel."

"I will be waiting for you. I have a special surprise when you arrive."

I'm looking forward to finding out. Can you give me a clue?"

"No, you will just have to wait. I love you."

"I love you too," As she gave him a kiss on the cheek.

Winton didn't want to be late so he headed to the regional airport. Carissa adequately insured, packed the vase, and continued coordinating the logistics. The estimated value of the vase was $375,000.00 dollars. Carissa paid $200K so she would make a nice profit of approximately $175K. This was a good profit for just answering the phone.

Just then, she heard the doorbell ring. She thought it was the logistics company. When she opened the door, there were officials from the regional airport.

"Ma'am, are you Carissa Covington?" the man asked politely.

"Yes, what's the matter?" She replied with concern.

"We are from the Dustin Regional Airport. The aircraft carrying your husband Winton Covington crashed. There were no survivors. I'm sorry for your loss." The man said in a calm voice.

Carissa was in shock. She could not believe her ears. Her husband was gone. She was now a widower. They hadn't even made it to their first year wedding anniversary. Her phone began to ring feverously. Everyone was calling trying to get more details. She just broke down and yelled with grief. Her thoughts were uncontrollable. Her parents arrived shortly attempting to comfort her but to no avail. It was a sad day. She couldn't help but think that she was supposed to be on that plane with her husband and now he is dead. She just didn't understand what was happening. Tragedy had come to visit her life in the most devastating way.

The funeral was a quiet ceremony with only family. Carissa mourned the loss of her husband. This tragedy turned her life upside down. She experienced so many different emotions throughout the grieving process. She took Winton's death very hard. Many at her husband's company were concerned about what was going to happen.

Weeks turned into months as each day brought a little less pain from her loss. She still cried from time to time but not as much as before. She knew she had to keep on living. She kept herself busy and engrossed into her work—it kept her mind occupied. Soon it had been almost a year since her husband's death. Winton crossed her mind from time to time as different things reminded her of him.

***

Jenifer called to check on her friend. She was supportive during this tragic point in Carissa's life.

"Carissa, how are you holding up?"

"I'm ok. Most days are good. I have to accept that death is part of life.

"Guess who will be in concern in a month?"

"Who," She replied curiously.

"Anthony Harrison. He will be performing here in town next month."

"Really, I haven't seen him in years. It's been almost two years I think."

Carissa hadn't heard Anthony's name in a long time. Her thoughts took her back to her time with him. She remembered all the details. She wondered how he was doing. It had been over two years since she last spoke or seen him. She lost contact after she told him she couldn't see him anymore. Carissa questioned her judgment. Did she really make the right decision? Does he care about me after all this time? Is he married? All these thoughts dominated her mind as she replayed the possibility of seeing him again.

"Do you want to go?"

"I'm not sure that is a good idea," Carissa replies.

"I know things didn't end well the last time you saw him. You have changed and I'm sure he has as well. Besides, it's just a concert."

"I will think about it."

"That's fair enough."

Jennifer had a point. It would be just a concert. However, Carissa wasn't sure if she was ready emotionally to see Anthony again. Ironically, seeing him in concert would be similar to the first time she saw Anthony perform at *Jake's*. This situation had a sense of déjà vu.

***

A lot had changes over the years since Anthony won the contest. He completed his first album and was on tour. He completed his twenty-six city US tour and began a ten-city tour through South America. Anthony took four months off to work on his second album. While in New York working on his album, he was sorting through some past emotions. He visited family and friends before beginning his second album tour in Europe, Africa, and Asia, and Australia.

The last song on his second album was a dedication song to the woman that had broken his heart. At the end of each show, he would sit and tell the audience how he got into the music industry and the background about the song.

[Ladies and gentlemen, I want to take a few

minutes before I close the show to tell you about my music career. I was studying to be an engineer but that wasn't my passion or dream. That's what my father wanted me to be. Things didn't work out financially in school so I ended up driving a delivery truck. I always wanted to sing so I stuck with it. I met a woman that changed my life but broke my heart. She gave me a piece of advice that her "Papa" had given her. 'Live your life for you, all others are just spectators.' That statement resonated with me for a long time until I sat down and wrote this song about that philosophy. I haven't seen the woman that inspired me to write this song and perhaps it's best that I don't. The song has helped me heal and grow. I hope that it will do the same for you. Live Your Life]

Anthony ended every concert the same way. Each time he told his story, he became a little stronger emotionally. Anthony still carried a 'torch' for Carissa in his heart. She was that special woman that crossed his path and changed his life. There were other women but he found himself drawn to her even after she had broken his heart.

***

Carissa wrestled with her thoughts and finally decided to go to the concert with Jennifer. This was the last show of Anthony's world tour. Appropriately, the tour would culminate in New York City. This was where it all started. Carissa and Jennifer reached the concert hall and found their VIP seats.

"These are great seats Jennifer."

Thanks, I figured you wanted to be close since you haven't seen Anthony in a long time."

"What are you up to Jen?"

"I'm innocent I tell you," she grinned.

Anthony came on stage and performed—putting on an amazing show. One song after the other, each song was a heartfelt collection of emotions, feelings, and desires. From ballads to spicy jam sessions, Anthony's music was a rollercoaster ride of excitement and entertainment.

He was down to the final number of the concert. Everyone expected his signature ending. He began the dialogue with the audience as he had done so many times before at other concerts. When he looked into the audience, he spotted Carissa. He was pleasantly surprised to see her at the concert. He gestured for security to allow her to come on stage.

"Everyone, I want you all to know there is something special happening here in NYC. This is my home and tonight I got a special homecoming surprise. My inspiration for the final song off my second album and always the last song of my concert is here tonight.

Carissa, will you come up here on stage with me? Here is the woman that I sing my last song about because she has always been a part of me. She doesn't know it but I fell in love with her years ago and I'm still in love with her," As Anthony gestured for security to allow her onstage.

Tears filled Carissa eyes at this point. She realized

she had always loved Anthony but allowed her family and social circles to dictate how she should live her life. Then, she remembered what her Papa had said: Live your life for you; all others are spectators.

By the end of the song, there wasn't a person still sitting. Many in the audience had tears of joy seeing Anthony and Carissa reunited. These two unlikely hearts became one once again.

Poetic Expression

I want to hear you perform.

I want to hear you present that side that you often hide, the side you put away, like that umbrella on a rainy turned sunny day.

Show those emotions, don't just tell me. I want to see what I can't hear, taste what I can't smell and feel what I can't touch.

Am I rambling along to my favorite song; or are you reading my thoughts that I didn't write down?

Now, I'm showing my emotions. Men do cry. You just don't see my tears. Weeping is not a weakness. It is that turning point toward healing; cleansing the soul and cutting the bounds of those emotional that hold me hostage.

I want to hear you perform, I want to hear you present that side that you often hide, the side you put away, like that umbrella on a rainy turned sunny day.

Whispering Questions

August 27, 2014

Do you feel what I feel as I breathe what you breathe?

Can you feel what I say?

Am I mysterious because I just walked into your life?

Did I make a lasting impression
without saying a word?

Am I looking through you with my eyes closed?

Do you hear my voice in a room filled with silence?

Do I make love to your mind more
than I do to your body?

Are your raw emotions exposed?

If I were your screenwriter, will
you be my leading lady?

If I rubbed the inside of your thigh from the
top of your knee, will you tell me to stop?

As my strong hands touch you, will you
be able to feel my gentle touch?

Does my warm breath on the back of
your neck give you goose bumps?

When our eyes meet, what does your mind tell you?

As my hands drive down the road of your womanly
curves and contours, will you enjoy the ride?

As our words and our thoughts continue
our mingling, does that make your juices
build, flow with a bit of tingling?

Do my words tease your mind's palette like a
small spoon full of your favorite dessert?

When I hold you in my arms, do you feel safe?

If I nibble on your ear lobes, does that
mean I'm hungry for you?

If I taste your juices, does that mean I'm thirsty too?

Did my words create a love scene
in your mind's movie?

Conclusion

The thrill ride and adventure has reached a logical stopping point. I hope you held on tightly, enjoyed the ride, and embraced the moment.